CW00539585

Meantime in Greenwich

Love, Laughter and Happily Ever After
Book 1

Hannah Keens

This edition published by:
Hartsmile Books, London 2024

First published in 2016

© Hannah Keens 2016

ISBN: 9781915421173

British Library Cataloguing in Publication Data. A catalogue record for
this book is available from the British Library.
Cover design: Get Covers

For my mother

Contents

Greenwich Mean Time

Mean solar time at the Greenwich meridian, internationally recognized as a standard time; abbreviated *GMT*.

— *Oxford English Dictionary*

Chapter One

So much for the trusty old London Underground. The Jubilee line train had been stuck for a sweltering half an hour while Stella McElhone checked and rechecked the time. When they eventually chugged into Westminster, the driver announced over a tinny-sounding tannoy that the train was terminating and the whole line was being suspended. Passengers were advised to change to the Circle and District lines. Determined not to spend another minute trapped below ground, Stella shot out of the train and legged it up the escalators, barely noticing the brutalist architecture in the deep well of the station. Once out of that austere environment, she bolted towards the River Thames, just in time to catch the river bus from Westminster Pier. It would take a good forty minutes, but short of an act of piracy, the boat would at least get her to Greenwich on time.

The impromptu summer-evening jaunt proved to be a delight, with the London skyline reeling past, only not quickly enough for her liking. Once the boat moved downriver from the London Eye, it took an age for St Paul's Cathedral and the Shard to pass from sight, but then the boat moved beneath Tower Bridge and at last gathered pace as it navigated the loops and bends of the river that separated north and south London.

When the twin domes of the old naval hospital hoved into view, Stella knew Greenwich was close. On arrival there, she disembarked and dashed along the pier into a lovely borough of south-east London. She ran towards the park, her dark hair swinging behind her. That evening, she was attending a night sky showing at the planetarium, with a lecture afterwards from a visiting astronomer. Her destination was only about half a mile away, but if she didn't get a move on, she'd be late and make a bad entrance.

At the other side of the leafy park, she reached a hill, graced with the seventeenth century Royal Observatory. This then, was the home of Greenwich Mean Time, by which the world had once set its clocks. The observatory resembled a domed palace, its red brick façade burnished by the evening sun. At the top of the hill, Stella stood back to avoid being flattened by a flood of boisterous schoolchildren surging past. Once certain there was no further risk of being trampled, she made her way to the main entrance and had her ticket scanned by an assistant who pointed her in the right direction.

In the courtyard, she paused to catch her breath. Because the observatory was on relatively high ground, she could see a fair amount of the London skyline that she'd just cruised past in the distance. Beneath her feet, she found the unassuming metal strip that represented the prime meridian, which marked nought degrees longitude. She couldn't resist taking a minute to place her feet either side of it, so she was standing with one foot in the east and one in the west.

When the novelty wore off, she headed for the planetarium, which stood in stark contrast to the buildings surrounding it, and the modern bronze monolith reminded her of a sawn-off telescope. Inside a light and airy reception area, Stella found her fellow attendees. Despite a few dozen people being present, the place was as quiet as an old library and she felt that even her clothes were too loud. Her pink jumper was positively shouting and drowning out a surprising number of outfits made from tweed. She peeled off her jumper and hung it over one arm. Who would wear tweed in this heat? And such pallor, even in July. These were not people who went outside in the daytime.

By the looks of things, there was no one here under fifty, let alone thirty, and she tried not to look as disappointed as she felt. Life in London was lonesome and she'd hoped to make some new acquaintances. It had been a mad rush to get here, but now she regretted not dawdling and saving herself from what was obviously going to be death by small talk. When a passing waiter came within arm's reach, she swiped a glass of red wine and clutched it for security. It wouldn't matter if she got purple teeth as it was unlikely she'd be smiling at anyone this evening.

One mouthful of wine – all right, three mouthfuls of wine – and she'd force herself to speak to someone. Apart from Ernie the doorman at her building, she hadn't spoken to anyone in real life for days, if not weeks. Fuelled by wine, she approached a trio on her left, which included an elegant blonde woman, who looked reasonably close to her own age. Next to her was a man with loopy brown hair, wearing a corduroy suit in a shade best described as quinoa. Finally, there was a woman clad in a puce knitted dress, complete with a wool scarf wrapped three times around her throat. Something about people interested in astronomy must attract them to warm clothing, which made sense if they spent a lot of their nights outside viewing the sky. Carefully, so as not to startle them, she made her approach.

'Greenwich is a lovely part of London, isn't it?' she said.

'If you like that sort of thing,' said the blonde woman, managing to peer down her nose at Stella, even though they were the same height. 'Now, if you'll excuse us.'

The woman ushered her two companions across the room towards a row of trestle tables covered with pretty

3

canapés. There, the three of them stood, not eating or even looking at the food, and continued their conversation unmolested.

This charming behaviour was not entirely unexpected. Stella had only been in the city for a few weeks but was already getting used to Londoners' way of not speaking to anyone, or looking at anyone, unless – or even if – their lives depended on it. She sipped her wine and looked about for other likely targets for her cringe-making opening gambits, but everyone was clustered in tightly drawn conversational knots that made it clear she wouldn't be welcome in any of them.

The prospect of standing about nursing a glass of wine for the next fifteen minutes was not especially appealing. Her best bet would be to lurk in the ladies and check her hair, but she could hardly spin that out for a whole quarter of an hour. Instead, she placed her glass on a nearby table and set off in search of the library.

Years ago, she'd discovered that the first Astronomer Royal had cast a horoscope to determine the best time for the construction of the Royal Observatory, and she wanted to see it in person. Imagine all those astronomers who loathed astrology doing their best work in a building conceived according to astrological principles. There was a copy of the chart on the observatory website, but it would be great to get a look at the real thing, assuming astrologers weren't barred from the library or forced to wear a bell around their necks or something.

An assistant informed her that the archives were held in another building at the opposite side of the park, which had closed some hours ago. Not to worry. Stella soon came up with another idea and made her way to the planetarium entrance, hoping to get in early and take her seat. Plan B was thwarted when she found the doorway barricaded with a red rope suspended over a bright yellow sign informing her that cleaning was in progress.

A quick listen revealed no hint of anyone hoovering.

Perhaps whoever was in there was quietly peeling chewing gum from underneath seats or removing whatever other sticky detritus schoolchildren were inclined to leave behind them. More likely the sign was just an oversight and the caretakers had long gone. Surely no one would mind if she crept in a bit early. A quick glance over one shoulder confirmed there was no one watching her, and even if anyone did spot her, she had a valid ticket, so it wasn't really trespassing, as such. Before she could change her mind, she stretched out a furtive hand to unhook the red rope.

'Breaking and entering?' said a voice from the dark void beyond. 'You could get six years for that. Fourteen if the judge doesn't like the cut of your jib.'

'Oh!' Stella flinched and withdrew her hand. 'But I haven't broken anything, or even entered, for that matter.'

'I know you haven't.' A man appeared from the darkened room and took the rope from her hand. 'Sorry, just kidding.'

'Very amusing,' said Stella. 'Best not give up the day job just yet. Look, I only wanted to get in ahead of time to avoid that lot.' She tilted her chin towards the other attendees. 'These drinks and nibbles things bring me out in a rash.' As if to prove the point, her face was now burning, partly from being caught red-handed and partly from being in close proximity to this good-looking man. He was tall, with pale blue eyes, nicely set off by a thatch of sandy hair. Even better, he was possibly the only other person present wearing clothes that looked like they'd been purchased in the twenty-first century: a blue cotton shirt, navy jumper and faded jeans. The jumper had a hole at the elbow, which was fraying badly. Was this the mark of a single man, or one married to a woman who took the view – quite rightly – that he could jolly well mend his own jumper, or was he just a man in his work clothes? Evidently, she'd disturbed the caretaker doing a last-minute tidy up before the show.

'Sorry,' he said. 'Where are my manners. Benedict Redman.'

He held out a calloused hand and she shook it. Hopefully, he'd not noticed her looking him up and down.

'Stella McElhone. Pleased to meet you.'

'The pleasure is mine. You don't sound local. Where are you from? The north-east?'

It was too complicated to say that she didn't really come from anywhere any more, so she opted for the short version.

'Originally from the north-east, yes. Durham. I'm here for a spot of flat-sitting. Well not *here*, here. I'm in London for flat-sitting purposes. I'm *here*, here for the Saturn lecture.'

If he'd noticed her babbling, he didn't let on. Impressively polite. Another point in his favour.

'I see,' he said. 'And do you have a particular interest in Saturn?'

Now was neither the time nor the place to discuss the fact that she was here to learn more about the vanishing of Saturn's rings and the effect that it may or may not have on people's lives. Many of her astrology clients were in their mid to late twenties and were fast-approaching their Saturn return, and she wasn't just interested for the sake of her clients, because this character-building planetary transit was one she was soon due to experience first-hand.

One of the more challenging planets, Saturn returned to the same point in people's birth-charts in their late twenties, again in their late fifties and for a third time in their late eighties. Mercifully, very few people had to suffer four Saturn returns. Aware that Benedict Redman was waiting for an answer, she cautioned herself not to babble again.

'Oh, well. You know. Not a particular interest in Saturn *per se*. At least no more than any other planet, really, and I'm just as interested in Uranus.' *Why* had she mentioned Uranus? What was wrong with her? 'They're all the same to me, planets. So, in conclusion, I'm just an interested bystander.'

The caretaker looked as though he was about to ask her

another question, but before he got a chance, he was beckoned by the snooty blonde woman.

'I'm sorry, Ms McElhone, it was lovely talking to you, but you'll have to excuse me. I hope you enjoy the lecture, and maybe we'll have a chance to speak afterwards?'

'I hope so.' After her not-so-stellar conversational performance, he'd no doubt keep well away from her if he had any sense.

Idly, she wondered what lay in his horoscope and whether she'd ever get the chance to find out. Obviously, it would be unsubtle to ask someone's sun sign, but she wasn't above a bit of sneaky interrogation to get birth details out of interesting people. He had the look and feel of an Aries: tall, fair, confident, friendly and charming, but as he was someone she'd only just met, it was unlikely to be his sun sign she was seeing, and most likely, he'd have an Aries ascendant. The zodiac sign rising over the horizon at birth was just like a front door: an outward portrayal to strangers of what might lie within. Sometimes, an ascendant was a good representation and sometimes completely misleading. In Stella's experience, many a glossy front door had opened to reveal an absolute slum, and she wasn't just referring to her flat-sitting career.

As there was no chance to quiz Benedict Redman just now, she observed him at a distance where the blonde woman was berating the poor man. Now, *she* was decidedly leonine, with quite a commanding presence. What she lacked in height, she made up for with her luxuriant mane, upswept to halo her face. Stella would bet her grocery money that this woman had a Leo ascendant. The man only folded his arms and listened attentively, not looking at all contrite. If this woman was his boss, then she felt rather sorry for him.

When a bell sounded, the crowd began moving towards Stella. Since the caretaker was still having his ear bent by the blonde woman, she unhooked the red rope herself, inched around the cleaning sign and walked into the planetarium. She headed for the point furthest from the door and parked herself in a reclining chair. Making sure her phone was switched off occupied a good couple of minutes and ensured she didn't have to make eye contact with anyone before the show started.

When everyone was seated, the lights dimmed and the room darkened, so she settled back, ready for a relaxing voyage through the universe. As the emerging night sky and the lulling voice of the commentator drew her forwards in space, she found herself slipping back in time to her childhood. To the time her parents had first taken her to a planetarium when she was eleven, where she'd sat in awed silence, watching the galaxies spread out overhead. It was one of the last times in her life that she'd been truly happy.

The show ended and Stella blinked in the rising lights. When her eyes refocused, she looked up to see Benedict Redman smiling over at her, also blinking. Beside him was the blonde woman, who gave him a sideways look. So, they weren't colleagues but a couple. It was too much to hope for, she supposed, to pick up the only man in the building who looked like he might have a pulse, let alone one who made hers race. She should have known he wouldn't be single. Just as well, really. It was pointless getting into anything with anyone when she'd be on the move again in a matter of months. That was the story of her life: she was always on the move again in a matter of months, or sometimes weeks.

Flat-sitting meant she had low overheads and could follow her heart at work instead of doing something she hated in order to pay high rents. On the downside, moving constantly from one end of the country to the other, and sometimes out of the country, also made it all but impossible to put down roots, to make friends or to maintain relationships. But if she was honest with herself, that suited her just fine. Not loving anyone meant not losing anyone ever again.

Reluctantly, she followed the other visitors back to the reception area where there were more drinks and nibbles. She was glad to get another drink after leaving most of her first glass, but she wasn't looking forwards to another attempt at small talk with the tweed brigade. At least they seemed more enthusiastic now they'd been in the planetarium, like children let out of school early, and there was a buzz of conversation instead of the deathly silence she'd walked into on arrival. She helped herself to another glass of red wine and took a good swig.

'I'd be careful of that if I were you, Ms McElhone.'

'What?'

She spun round to see that Benedict Redman had escaped from his blonde companion. She smiled, but tried to do it without using any teeth, knowing they'd be only three shades lighter than the wine itself.

'The Saturn Committee organised their own wine,' he said, angling his head towards a group of men standing nearby, deep in conversation. 'The skinflints could use the leftovers to strip back the floorboards. Go on, spill a drop on the floor and watch it eat the varnish.'

She laughed, showing all her purple teeth. 'It can't be that bad. Besides, I couldn't pretend to know the first thing about wine and only know what I like.'

'And what do you like?'

'Well, it needs to be red. Or, it can be white. Not pink though. Except in an emergency, of course.'

'Naturally. Any port in a storm, eh?' He winked at Stella, who laughed overly hard at the mild pun.

'I suppose I'm not that choosy!'

'I'll remember that. Might be useful if I'm ever down on my luck with the ladies!'

'Don't make me laugh.' What a nerve, when his other half was standing only fifteen feet away. And who even said *ladies* any more? It made him sound about ninety.

9

'Speaking of which,' he said, 'I'd better get a move on. There's one lady-in-waiting who's not going to wait any longer.'

With that, Benedict Redman returned to the frowning blonde woman. Honestly, some men. Well, Stella had not come here on a manhunt but to find out more about the physical aspects of Saturn. In astrology, Saturn stood for rules and boundaries, no doubt represented by the colourful rings that circled the planet.

Stella loved working out how what went on in the heavens was reflected down on earth. She'd been thrilled to learn how the ancients had described this correspondence between the celestial and the terrestrial with 'as above, so below'. There was no longer any need to actually look at the physical stars to work out horoscopes as she had a two-inch-thick ephemeris that listed all the movements of the planets at any given time on any given day. Much loved and well used, it was dog-eared with many loose pages and filled with highlights, underlinings and sticky notes. Her laptop could whizz up a horoscope in a second, and she had various apps on her phone that were just as speedy, but she liked to feel the connection to the stars and the planets, to understand them in their wider context, so she often made horoscopes the old-fashioned way, by referring to her ephemeris, making minute mathematical calculations and drawing her birth charts by hand.

So familiar was she with planetary cycles that if push came to shove, she could work out the ascendant and the approximate planetary positions in her head without breaking a sweat. This wasn't remotely useful in real life – apart from being a good party trick on the rare occasions she actually attended any parties – but it did mean she was able to analyse people almost instantly armed with the smallest piece of information about their date and time of birth. More importantly, it meant that she had an innate understanding of planetary movements and could see in her mind's eye how they stood in relation to one another.

Meantime in Greenwich

After loitering with her glass of wine for ten minutes, it was a relief when the bell sounded and they were ushered into a side room set aside for the lecture. While she probably knew more about astronomy than the average person in the street, Stella was a total novice in a place like this and she'd be lucky if she understood a tenth of what was said. Greenwich held a revered status in astronomy circles, and she had no plans to reveal that astrology was her sole reason for being here. Cowardly of her, she knew, but she had no desire to be laughed out of any more academic events. The laughter would be polite, but all the more humiliating for that. So, she would drink no more wine, sit near the back and not, under any circumstances, ask even one tiny question.

Chapter Two

Benedict Redman approached the lectern. Evidently, the professor was late so the caretaker was about to announce that the lecture had been postponed due to the professor being ill-disposed on account of his leather elbow patches needing to be reinforced or something.

'Good evening, everyone,' he said, pushing up his threadbare jumper to reveal tanned and sinewy arms. 'Thank you all for coming this evening and for welcoming a stranger into your midst.' Polite laughter rippled around the room. 'For those who don't know me, I'm Benedict Redman, Professor of Astrophysics at the University of... well, no need to remind you all.'

At this point, he beamed at Stella, who was busy shrinking down in the back row, appalled that she'd mistaken the astronomy professor for the planetarium caretaker. She thanked her lucky stars that she hadn't tried to find out his birthday.

A large screen lit up behind Professor Redman and he proceeded to expound his latest theories on Saturn's vanishing rings. It was mind-boggling to think of these vast bands extending into space. Her father had tried to teach her the scale of the rings by imagining Earth as a tiny blue

and green car driving round a circular motorway
surrounding Saturn. If memory served, he'd calculated that
it would take a year-and-a-half of non-stop driving at the
national speed limit to complete a single lap of the smallest
ring. Although hundreds of thousands of miles wide, the
rings were only a few feet deep and every dozen or so years,
thanks to a weird optical illusion, they appeared to slip out
of view. Since Saturn affected society as much as the
individual, Stella had a pet theory that the apparent fading
of Saturn's own boundaries coincided with the periodic
loosening of social rules and mores. Beyond this regular
vanishing trick, Professor Redman went on to mention that
the rings, which were mainly ice particles, were also being
pulled into the planet so they would truly disappear
altogether in a hundred million years or so.

Stella wondered what this prospect would mean for
human beings in terms of rules and regulations, but also the
physical aspects ruled by Saturn: skin, for one, and bones
and teeth for another. Perhaps humans (assuming they were
still a thing by then) would evolve to no longer need skin,
bones and teeth and instead become stationary blobs with
no need to move about. Perturbed by the idea, she shook
these idle notions away and tried to concentrate on the talk
instead.

Professor Redman was now showing a slide covered with
complicated equations. While these squiggles meant nothing
to Stella, they did seem to excite the other members of the
room to an inordinate degree. She had hoped to spend the
evening immersed in her favourite subject, surrounded by
people who knew more about the stars than she ever would,
but this was turning into a very dry talk, and if anyone here
felt any real passion for the planets, rather than equations, it
was not immediately obvious to her.

Of course, her own interest in the planets came from
her parents, who were very different people to those in this
room. When Stella was born, her parents had seen a
shooting star as they held their baby girl up to the window,

and that inspired them to call her after a star. They'd pored over books listing odd-sounding names for stars and some with just numbers, which had struck them as a dreadful waste of an opportunity, until they settled on Stella, the Latin word for star.

From being an infant, one or other of her parents had held her up to the open garret window, wrapped in a snug blanket to soak up the rays of the stars in the cool night air. On crisp winter nights, when the skies were black and punctured with silver holes, she would snuggle in her parents' arms as they pointed out the stars and taught her their names.

From being tiny, Stella could name the major constellations and the phases of the moon. She loved the stars for their mystery and their beauty, disappearing in the morning light and appearing magically in the night sky. When she got older, Stella's father told her that the universe was getting bigger all the time, that more and more stars kept appearing. When Stella wanted to know why, her father, perhaps at a loss for a scientific explanation, told her that they were new souls. Whenever someone on earth died and went to heaven, their soul became a new star. Stella found this both sad and beautiful, and wondered whether all the stars she could see nearest to earth were recently departed souls.

Not long before she turned twelve, the McElhone family had left Durham and moved to Wiltshire to be closer to Stonehenge. On her twelfth birthday, her parents gave her a telescope and she looked forwards to autumn and the dark nights so she could spend longer with her beloved skies before being parcelled off to bed. Not that she minded early nights because she loved her new bedroom with its brass bedstead and patchwork quilt. After living for so long in a city flat, it was luxurious having a whole house to themselves, with a garden they could use whenever they liked. She loved to sit in her window seat, with the stars above shining down on her, keeping her and her family safe. Only, things had not quite worked out that way.

Before she could get too maudlin, Benedict's voice rose, pulling her out of her reverie.

'...and as Saturn's rings start to vanish before our eyes, let's hope the same thing doesn't happen to our research grants.'

Relieved the lecture was finally over, Stella joined in the applause that signalled the end of the talk. The woman in the wool dress (still complete with tightly wound scarf) took to the lectern, thanked Professor Redman for his presentation and asked the guests to stay behind for further socialising. Now was the time for Stella to slip away. She couldn't possibly hold her own in a conversation with any of these people, who'd want to talk about particle physics, quantum theory and who knew what else besides. They'd not be remotely interested in discussing the magic worked by the planets as they shone down on earth and its inhabitants.

She gathered her jumper and her bag, aiming to leave quietly, and was trying to stuff her arms into her sleeves without much luck. Cursing herself for not realising they were inside out, she reversed out, ready to start the procedure again when a hand plucked the jumper from her, grazing her skin. A bolt of lightning shot up her arm and she reddened as she looked up into the crinkled, good-natured eyes of Benedict Redman. He shook her jumper to right the sleeves and held it out for her.

'Can't leave you to struggle by yourself, can we?'

'Thank you.' She grimaced, mortified that she'd been bested by her own knitwear. 'Your talk was...' What word to use without causing offence? *Amazing* would sound sarcastic, as would *fantastic*. 'Your talk was really... eye-opening. Why didn't you tell me you were giving the lecture?' No need to mention that she'd mistaken him for the caretaker.

'I assumed you'd seen my name on your ticket.'

Or on the banner over the door, or in fact, on any of the

several posters plastered around the place that she now noticed. How embarrassing.

'Oh, I never read tickets. I mean, who does?' Stella organised herself into her jumper and gazed up at him through her eyelashes. 'Sorry, but I have to leave. I've… got to be up very early in the morning.' Yes, because astrologers were famous for needing the morning light to do their work. Her first readings were typically never before midday.

'What a shame, I was hoping to get to know you better over the paint-stripper. It's not that often I get to spend time in such delightful company. And it's not often that I get to spend time with anyone not dressed in tweed.'

He almost whispered this last part in her ear. Stella smirked, and not just because her blonde rival was dressed in a monochrome tweed skirt suit. Couture tweed that probably cost more than the average astrologer earned in six months, but tweed nonetheless. He didn't so much as glance over his shoulder at the woman, who was quite openly giving Stella daggers.

'You know,' he said, 'if it's not too short notice, I'll be here again on Saturday morning, faffing about with one of the telescopes. But afterwards, if it's fine, we could take a walk in the park and then grab some lunch, if you fancy it?'

Stella fancied it very much indeed but couldn't just blurt that out. She turned herself slightly so the blonde woman was no longer in her field of vision. That woman mustn't be his wife or he wouldn't be so blatantly chatting up a virtual stranger, let alone asking her out. She slid her eyes down to his ring finger. Bare. And no sign of any pale skin suggesting he'd just taken his ring off. It wouldn't be the first time she'd fallen for that one. But if there ever had been a ring, and he'd taken it off, he'd taken it off a long time ago. Due diligence carried out, she was satisfied he was not married and that the blonde woman was probably just another astronomer or someone on the Saturn Committee, so she accepted.

'That would be fine,' she said, but her happiness was

short-lived as the blonde woman was now bearing down on them.

'I'm sorry to interrupt, Benedict—'

'Yet you manage to look far from sorry, Miranda.'

Miranda frowned. Despite having only seen her briefly this evening, Stella had already witnessed at least four different frowns. Perhaps she practised them at home in front of a mirror.

'Don't be exasperating, Benedict. There are people who need to discuss important matters with you – think of your next research grant.'

She lowered her voice at the end of the sentence and it was clear that this Miranda was so posh that she found it vulgar to talk about money. Well, Stella didn't want stand in the way of important grant-related discussions and would shove off, but not before securing the proffered date.

'It was lovely meeting you, Professor Redman.'

'And you, Stella. I'll see you here on Saturday. Does eleven suit?'

'Eleven's fine. See you then. And in the meantime, best of luck with the expansion – both universal and financial.'

He didn't reply and merely raised a hand, which struck her as rather dismissive. Perhaps she'd just dropped a clanger without realising it. Was the universe still expanding? Might it even be contracting? Too late to worry now. Stella eased her way past people talking solemnly and sipping wine. Quite a few of them even managed not to cringe while doing so. At least those stiff upper lips were good for something.

Outside, it had grown dark and Stella booked an Uber driver to come and collect her. While waiting, she paused to search for the stars. Because Greenwich was so near to central London, there was too much glare to do any real stargazing, but there was a certain beauty in the imitation stars provided by the bright lights spread in a twinkling wall across the other side of the River Thames. Her phone pinged to advise that the car was approaching. As it drew to a halt, she checked that the licence plate matched the one shown on the app, then climbed gratefully into the back seat.

'Been star-spotting?' asked the driver.

'Kind of…'

'Do you mind if I listen to the radio?'

'Not at all.'

It was a cricket match but even that was preferable to thirty minutes of debating the vagaries of the London weather when she could while away the time processing some of the memories that had come to the surface during the planetarium show.

Stella and her parents had barely been in Wiltshire for a month when she came home one afternoon to find their lovely new house locked and empty. A cold feeling enveloped her, but as she didn't really know anyone in the area, or what to do or where to go, she sat on the step and waited.

When a police car drove up the road, all the blood drained from her limbs, leaving her glued to the cold step. A police officer bent down and patted her shoulder, speaking softly to her. But Stella didn't want to hear – wouldn't hear. She put her hands over her ears and screamed, something deep inside telling her that if she didn't hear it, then it couldn't be true.

A nice lady with the police officer drew her into a car and took her away from home. Of course, it wasn't really home. She still thought of Durham as home. They'd barely settled in to the south-west and she'd yet to make any friends at school where most of the kids laughed at the new girl's accent.

The lady drove her miles away to a children's home. When she'd been put to bed in a room with two other girls, a doctor arrived and gave her an injection. She still remembered the cold, sharp feeling in her arm, and then she remembered nothing – not the ensuing days and weeks, and not even her parents' funeral. Their house was rented and they had nothing to leave and no will, so they'd been given a council cremation. It was many months before Stella was well enough to ask about their ashes. She was given forms to fill out, but to no avail. Her parents' ashes were nowhere to be found, so she'd never had a chance to say goodbye to them in life or after their death.

Stella would sit quietly all day and then spend all night looking out of the window at the night sky. Unbeknownst to the carers at the children's home, she was searching for the new stars that were her mother and father. She searched for their souls, certain that they were somehow looking down on her and looking after her. Eventually, a box of her belongings turned up, and she pulled out her telescope, hugging it to her chest. One of the carers put a small table in Stella's room near to the window.

'It's going to be a long journey back to daylight for you, Stella, but this might be a start.'

Within a matter of weeks, her telescope had been stolen from her, and that was the very least of the bad things that began happening to her. The newly orphaned girl had no family, and it soon became clear that no other family wanted her. Everyone wanted babies and toddlers: a blank slate on which to project themselves.

At eighteen, she'd been pushed out of care to fend for herself. With no clue about where to turn, she'd gone to the council offices where an officious woman told her in no uncertain terms that there was no chance of her qualifying for accommodation, but she had at least pointed her in the direction of a flat-sitting service.

'Course, they won't want you, on account of your age and lack of references, to say nothing of your background, but you'll have to make the best of a bad job.'

Armed only with a half-hearted reference from college and one from the manager at the children's home, Stella had embarked on an unsteady flat-sitting career. She'd not done very well at school and had to resit her GCSEs at college. If she was honest, she had very little use for academic learning. In particular, maths had been a total waste of time, and the only use she'd ever found for logarithms was in calculating exact planetary positions for a specific time of birth.

Her early days of flat-sitting had been hardest as she did odd days here and there, earning what she could by selling birth charts online and interpreting them for clients willing to pay — clients who weren't too worried that their consulting astrologer was often sitting on a coach, or in a coach station, with purple crescent moons beneath her eyes. She filled the days between flat-sitting assignments by travelling on long-distance coaches and sleeping as best she could, her life's belongings taking up no more than a rucksack.

It was little wonder she was rootless. Her sun and moon were conjunct in the fourth house, right on the nadir of her birth chart. The fourth house represented home and roots, while the fast-moving moon led to restlessness, and the close presence of the sun amplified its effects. Forever on the move, with no home to call her own, she was hollow with loneliness, but within less than a decade, she'd built up a good collection of references and had many repeat customers, which made it easier to find longer flat-sitting contracts that allowed her to feel a little more settled. She seldom met the homeowners though, and hers was an isolated existence, with no one to greet her when she came home or to wish her well when she went out.

In all these years, she'd failed to come to terms with the fact that she had no family, that her parents had died and that with a sudden, cruel stroke of fate, she was orphaned and alone, with no one between her and the precipice that was the rest of the world. Safe in the heart of her family, she'd never had cause to think about sadness, horror or loneliness. Now all three were ever-present. She'd grown up in the care of people who were paid to take care of her. Some of them were kind and some of them less so. None of them ever stayed in post long, so her life was never constant and she'd carried this pattern into adulthood. Now, she was truly alone in the vast universe, and being in a city as large as London only made it seem more so.

The driver coughed to get her attention and she was surprised to see they'd pulled up outside her apartment block. With its red-brick mansion flats, embellished with cupolas, wrought-iron balconies and bay windows piped in white plaster, the building resembled a tall gingerbread house.

'Here we go. NW8.' The cabbie whistled. 'You must be well-to-do, living in St John's Wood, or your folks are, at any rate.'

'No, not me, and not my folks either. I'm just flat-sitting for a few months. So, your tip won't be enough to retire on, I'm sorry to say.' She got her phone out, ready to add a tip.

'All right by me, love. You take care now.'

She smiled at this unexpected kindness. The driver was a total stranger, and she knew it was just a turn of phrase, but he'd sounded genuine. So rarely did anyone show her any affection that when they did, she was like a dog at broth. She let herself into the main door of the building and walked into the lobby, pleased to see that Ernie was on duty behind the desk in his cubby-hole near the lift. The elderly porter always had a kind word to say when she was coming and going, which was something she'd sorely missed in her life. Ernie was busy pouring hot chocolate from his flask, and on seeing her, raised his tin mug in a toast and enquired after her evening.

While she stood chatting to Ernie, the sweet perfume of his drink set off a craving for hot chocolate and once upstairs she made herself a mugful. Out on her small balcony, she looked down at the dark, tree-lined street below her. Although the night was still warm, she shivered, glad of her warm and comforting drink, but even that didn't stop her feeling alone in a strange city and all alone in the world.

At times like these, she often thought about visiting her birthplace in Durham. She'd been putting it off for so many years but now that her Saturn return was approaching, perhaps it was the right time to look to her roots and start to come to terms with all that she'd lost. Deep down, she knew it would be impossible to move on with her life until she did so.

She'd lost touch with her old school-friends in Durham and she had no extended family there. Even so, visiting some of her old haunts might bring her closer to her past. The staff at the children's home had always discouraged her from visiting her birthplace, and she'd not pressed the matter with them. There was no one holding her back now, but did she possess the strength to go and stand outside her family home, and was she strong enough to face it alone?

Chapter Three

On Saturday morning, Stella bought the largest coffee she could find and made her way across Greenwich Park where groups of kids (and adults) were having a kickabout, families with small children were flying kites, and couples were walking hand in hand. It was a lovely park and Stella was pleased to see so many happy lives around her, even if it did increase her sense of loneliness. By the time she made it up the hill to the observatory, she'd finished drinking her coffee and was searching for a bin to dispose of the empty cup.

'There's a bin behind you, but you could more easily fit the bin in the cup than the other way around.'

Stella looked up to see a familiar face smiling down at her. A knot unloosened itself in her stomach. It wouldn't have surprised her at all if he'd not turned up.

'Hello, Benedict. Still working on the comedy routine?'

'When I can. You came then.'

'Evidently, and who is this handsome young man?'

Beside the professor was a bespectacled little boy with brown hair and brown eyes. Dimples winked in his chubby cheeks – a sure sign of either a Libran ascendant or Venus in the first house. Under her scrutiny, he blushed and hid behind his father's legs.

'This is my son, Daniel. He's a huge fan of the planetarium.'

'Hello, Daniel,' she said. 'I'm a huge fan of the planetarium, too.'

On hearing this, the little boy crept back into view. 'Are you coming in with us?'

Stella didn't know how to answer this question. Labouring under the impression that this was a date, she'd not really factored in spending the morning with a little kid, and she didn't want to muscle in on what now appeared to be dad-and-son quality time. But what kind of man fetched his son on a date, let alone a first date? Unless she'd woefully misunderstood what today was about. But she was confident that she hadn't got hold of the wrong end of the stick as Mercury wasn't retrograde at the moment and everything was rosy in Neptune's sea garden right now.

'Of course Stella is coming with us, Daniel. I explained that earlier.' Benedict looked up. 'I told Daniel about you on the train on our way here. He was supposed to be going camping this weekend but the camp leader tested positive for Covid this morning, so that put paid to that. I thought a trip to the planetarium might make up for the disappointment. Apologies for not forewarning you, only it didn't occur to me to ask for your phone number the other night.'

'Don't worry and please don't feel obliged to include me. I can easily entertain myself.'

'We wouldn't hear of it. Come on, planetarium for three it is.'

Benedict took his son's hand and together they headed into the planetarium and settled down for the show. Stella looked at the little boy's rapt face as he stared up at the night sky. Astronomy must be in the blood. Well, this wasn't her strangest first date by a long chalk, but it was certainly up there. She tried not to think about the man who'd once invited her on a date as a pretext to having her star in an 'art' film he was making. Stella hadn't paid much attention during art classes at school, but even she knew when something was definitely not art and had made a suitably swift exit.

When the planetarium show finished, Daniel was already up on his feet, crossing his legs and bobbing up and down.

'Daddy, I need a wee.'

'Come on, son. We won't be long, Stella,' said Benedict. 'Shall we meet you outside?'

Stella followed at a more leisurely pace. After a few minutes, Daniel emerged from the gents with his shirt and jumper tucked into his pants. Benedict bent down to straighten him up.

'Well, I don't know about anyone else,' he said, 'but I could do with something to eat. What does everyone fancy?'

While Stella had been looking forwards to a romantic bistro lunch for two, now that was out, it seemed churlish not to let the kid choose.

'I'm easy,' she said. 'Daniel, what would you like to eat?

'Burger,' said the little boy, without hesitation, beaming and showing a mouthful of milk teeth with two missing in the front. 'And I bet you want a burger too.'

'Dan-i-el,' said his father. 'Stella can choose for herself. Not everyone is as keen on burgers as you are.'

Stella grinned. 'My staple diet, given half a chance. So lead me to the burger joint of your choosing.'

'Would the West End take you too far out of your way?'

'As a matter of fact, I was on my way up there next to see a couple of films, so that works well for me.'

She'd thought it wise to have something planned for the afternoon in case she needed an excuse to leave and had come across an indie cinema showing a double bill of two of her favourite weather disaster movies.

Benedict took his son's hand and they walked through Greenwich Park to the river bus. It was a lot slower than the Tube, but much more exciting for a visiting six-year-old boy. Within the hour, they were seated at a window table in a restaurant just off Soho, ordering burgers, fries and chocolate milkshakes while London fizzed past.

When they'd finished eating, Stella glanced at her phone. 'Well, thank you for lunch, Benedict, and it was lovely to meet you, Daniel, but I'd best start making tracks if I'm to get to the pictures on time.'

'My pleasure.' Benedict stood up to see her off. 'I'm giving another lecture during the week in South Kensington. I don't suppose you'd like to come along?'

Did she really want to sit through another dry-as-dust astronomy lecture? Not particularly. But she did want to see more of the person giving the lecture, so one more night of equations would be a small price to pay.

'Er… yes, I'd like that. Thank you.'

'Let me have your number and I'll be in touch with the details. He unlocked his phone and handed it over while she typed in her number.

'There you go. Well, I'd better get a move on.'

She shrugged on her jumper and made her way outside, father and son waving at her as she left. Stella really didn't know what to think. Professor Redman was incredibly attractive, but he had a young son, which was new news. There was still a bit of a question mark over this Miranda woman, but it seemed unlikely that she was the boy's mother. Daniel didn't look at all like his father or Miranda. He was dark and they were both fair, so the boy's mother must be dark-haired and dark-eyed. According to her admittedly vague recollection from school biology, there was something to do with recessive genes that meant two blue-eyed people couldn't have a brown-eyed baby. Or maybe it was the other way around. As she'd paid no more attention to science than she had art, or any other subject come to that, it was impossible to be sure. Still, in all likelihood, Miranda wasn't Daniel's mother, so she could go to this lecture with a clear-ish conscience.

But that same conscience insisted on pointing out that Miranda might just as easily be a more recent addition to the family. Stella had hoped she was just someone from his work. Only slightly ashamed of herself, after meeting Benedict for the first time, she'd thoroughly scoured the university website and searched for a Miranda, but there was no sign of anyone by that name. If only she could just ask Benedict, but it was a bit early in the day for any kind of defining-the-relationship conversation. Plus, it wasn't even as if he'd invited her on a second date. He'd only invited her to his lecture, mistakenly thinking that she had a genuine interest in his work. Either that, or given how boring the last lecture was, he was short on numbers and trying to boost his audience.

Stella got ready for the date/lecture with special care. She looked at herself in the mirror and smoothed an orange tunic over her white linen trousers. Deck shoes completed her ensemble and she tied her hair up loosely, leaving a few strands to fall around her face. It wasn't a tweed suit, but it was just about formal enough for an evening lecture.

She'd almost changed her mind when Benedict texted her the lecture details a few days ago. Not even a phone call. That tipped the scale in favour of this not being a romantic assignation but a purely practical one. In his innocence, he probably thought he was doing her a favour.

It had been overcast all day, so just in case the night turned chilly, Stella pulled a soft cream wrap around her shoulders. The wrap had belonged to her mother and was in the precious box of belongings sent to the children's home. Her mother had crocheted it for her wedding. Not a good idea, thought Stella, unwinding the wrap and deciding it was not that cold after all.

Alighting from the Tube at South Ken, Stella was surprised by a throng of children dressed as characters from Peter Pan and had to swerve to avoid two miniature pirates chasing an even tinier Tinkerbell.

27

'Sorry, love,' said a breathless mother trying to catch her unruly offspring.

When she arrived at the institute where the lecture was taking place, Benedict was waiting on the steps and her heart flipped at the sight of him. No sign of the scruffy jumper this time. Instead, he was wearing a beautifully cut navy suit with a blue shirt and tie. He smiled and ran down the steps to greet her.

'Thanks for coming. I'm pleased you could make it. You're nice and early, so you should be able to nab the best seat. Come on, let me show you in.'

Together, they went into the old building and climbed to a large room at the top of a marble staircase. The lecture room had a high, vaulted ceiling and the whole place smelled of old wood and even older books. Stella settled into what appeared to be a repurposed church pew and watched Benedict while he organised his projector and checked his notes. Gradually, the room filled up around her. It was a relief that there were no refreshments this time, so at least she was spared from having to make polite conversation with strangers.

An untidy-looking man slid into the pew next to her and Stella slid away from him so she ended up jammed against the wall. So much for nabbing the best seat. Scrutinising him from the side of her eye, she was convinced she'd seen him before. When he removed his hat and his loopy brown hair tumbled out, she recognised him as the quinoa corduroy man from the night at the planetarium. Another glutton for punishment.

Benedict crossed the room and dimmed the lights before returning to his projector. As he turned on the slides, Stella prepared herself to look interested, but was disappointed to see that it was the same presentation she'd seen at Greenwich. It had been bad enough sitting through it the first time. Why would Benedict invite her to see the same presentation again? Judging by the number of empty seats, her theory about him making up the numbers was looking increasingly likely.

She was thrown out of her musing when she heard Benedict saying, 'Isn't that right, Stella?'

'Er, yes,' she mumbled. 'Yes it is.' What had she just agreed to? Hopefully not a third repeat of this lecture. She tried to pay more attention to the rest of the talk, but she was never good at watching re-runs, no matter how fetching the presenter.

At the end, there was a question-and-answer session. It was astonishing how the people in the audience seemed intent on besting Benedict. Every question was a challenge to his authority, but he dealt with each one easily and charmingly, never allowing anyone to put one over on him, but also never making anyone feel as though they'd lost. Quite the diplomat, so he must have something Libran about him. Either that, or a well-placed Venus.

After the questions, people started to filter out, and a few gravitated towards Benedict to pick his brain further. Stella wondered what to do. She'd been to the lecture as per the invitation, and now that it was over, she should probably go. She'd started to gather her belongings when Benedict appeared at her side.

'Sorry, Stella, can you give me ten minutes, then I'll be ready and we can go on somewhere?'

'No problem.'

She put her bag back at her side and checked her phone to see if she had any new client appointments. Summer could be a bit slow sometimes, what with people going on holiday or spending their hours doing outdoorsy things. At this rate, she'd have to do a bit of online advertising – always a double-edged sword as it was hard to bring in just the right number of customers without overwhelming herself. She'd give it another day or two and hopefully some of her regulars would be back off their hols soon.

'You're wasting your time, you know.'

The untidy-looking man was addressing her and she turned to look at him.

'Excuse me?'

He tipped his head towards Benedict. 'With him. You're wasting your time, and it's not really fair on the ankle-biter, is it? Getting him all upset for nothing. And Miranda won't be best pleased either.'

Stella looked at the man long and hard. Underneath his loopy brown hair was a face that looked as though someone had recently slept in it. As well as recalling him from the planetarium, she recognised that face only too well from the staff page on the university website. The photo looked about ten years out of date, but there was no mistaking that hair. He was another professor, who worked in the same field as Benedict and obviously knew him well enough to know that Miranda would not be best pleased about Stella being involved with him. Perhaps Benedict and Miranda were married after all, but recently estranged. Whatever the relationship was, there was definitely something there, and having seen Miranda in action, 'not best pleased' had to be something of an understatement – that woman could frown for England. Clearly, the pair of them were going through a difficult patch and Stella getting in their way wasn't helping at all.

Seeing that Benedict was engrossed with a gaggle of elderly astronomy groupies, she squeezed past the quinoa corduroy man – who, despite wanting shot of her, made no effort to move out of her way – then she crept out of the room, ran down the staircase, out of the door and arrived at the station, panting. Why was it that doing the right thing made her head feel a lot better but did the absolute opposite for her heart? She bypassed the Tube station and stopped at a kiosk to buy the biggest tub of ice cream available.

When Stella let herself through the outside door to her building and walked towards the lift, she saw Ernie's eyes travel to her tub of ice-cream, but he was kind enough not to mention it.

'Evening, Stella. You look as pretty as a summer flower in that get-up, if you don't mind my saying so.'

'Not at all, Ernie. It's very kind of you to say so.'

The porter was eighty if he was a day, so Stella really didn't mind at all and was grateful to him for not asking how she was, or whether she'd had a good evening, or any other awkward question that might set her chin quivering.

Her flat – hers temporarily, at any rate – was on the fifth floor of a sprawling mansion block on Abbey Road. The flat itself was quite small but very well appointed, with a huge bay window along with French doors that led to the balcony. She couldn't imagine what the flat must have cost its owner, but she was glad to have such luxurious quarters for a while. Her father would have loved it here as he'd been a huge fan of the Beatles. When she was little, he'd shown her the *Abbey Road* album, with the Beatles striding over the zebra crossing outside their recording studio. She felt a little closer to her father, being next to a landmark that would have meant so much to him.

Immediately she'd locked the door behind her, Stella threw down her bag, and changed into PJs and fluffy socks. She picked out the biggest spoon she could find in the kitchen drawer and peeled the lid off her ice-cream. She'd scoff the lot and push Professor Benedict Redman and his snooty Miranda out of her mind. After a couple of mouthfuls of vanilla, she retrieved her phone from her bag to see what was on TV and spotted that she had a voicemail. It must have come while she was on the Tube. She sighed, licked her spoon and pressed the button to listen to the message. It was from Benedict, who sounded remarkably cross.

'Stella? Benedict here. Where did you get to? I said I'd

only be ten minutes. Sincere apologies if that was too long to wait. I'd hoped we could go for something to eat. Daniel's safe and sound at home with Miranda. Look, when you get home, please call me. I don't understand what's going on, but I'm still in London, so call me back, and we can go somewhere for a late supper if–'

Without listening to the end, Stella deleted the message. Unbelievable! Even mentioning his wife and son while berating her for leaving him in the lurch. Obviously, he was the worst sort of man and she'd done well to get out of his way before it was too late. She dug angrily into her ice cream. Although she hadn't managed to find her favourite fudge, or her second-favourite chocolate, vanilla wasn't too awful and would just have to do. When the phone rang again, she jammed the spoon into the tub. Well! He was obviously annoyed because she'd wrecked his plans, and he'd be even more annoyed when she gave him a piece of her mind and told him that he couldn't behave like this and expect to get away with it. On the third ring, she snatched up the phone.

'Professor Redman,' she said. 'What can I do for you?'

'You can tell me why you ran out on me. One minute you were there, and the next, you'd vanished. And please stop calling me Professor.'

'Please accept my deepest apologies, Professor. I came for the lecture as requested and then decided to go home. While I am interested in the stars, I have zero interest in getting involved with married men. Please refrain from calling again. Goodnight.'

With that, she hung up, prised the spoon free from the tub and rammed a spoonful of ice cream into her mouth. The phone began to ring again immediately. Stella rejected the call then turned off her phone and removed the battery for good measure. At last, she could get back to her ice cream and TV. But her heart wasn't in it any more, so she stuffed the tub into the freezer and went to bed instead, then lay awake wondering how she could have been so stupid, and what kind of man would involve his little boy in this kind of subterfuge.

Chapter Four

After her unexpectedly early night, Stella awoke not long after dawn. It was a bit early for breakfast so she squeezed some oranges to keep her going for the time being. While drinking her juice, she decided to see if the planets could shed some light on her so-called love life. A quick check on recent planetary transits might help her to navigate some of what was going on. This was something she tried to avoid wherever possible because there were so many cautionary tales of astrologers suffering from acute transititis, who could barely make a cup of tea without consulting an ephemeris first. So, although she didn't like to use astrology to explain away painful episodes, today she would make an exception.

She pulled out her ephemeris for the twenty-first century. Unlike her ephemeris for the twentieth century, this one was in a reasonably good state of repair. It was a simple matter to find the page for this week and to track the planets' movements for the past few days.

The emotional moon had just crossed into her seventh house, where it opposed Mars, the planet that represented a man in a woman's chart. She laughed in spite of herself. It was all there. A man signified by the red planet. A red man.

In particular, one Benedict Redman, sitting right opposite the house of marriage.

By rights, there should be a challenge from Saturn, it being the planet of blockages and boundaries, and a difficult aspect to Saturn would represent the barrier of Benedict's marriage. But there was nothing there. Oddly, Venus was all loved up with Neptune the deceiver, who was renowned for bringing confusion to everything he touched with his foggy fingers, often making it impossible to separate fact from fiction.

Something didn't add up, though. She'd always prided herself on being able to visualise complex planetary transits in her mind's eye. Perhaps she was losing her touch and should work it all out on paper in case she'd missed a trick. Yet, she was sure she hadn't.

No matter how tempted she was by Benedict Redman, he was clearly involved with this Miranda woman, plus there was a child in the mix, and Stella was not that sort of girl. She could never hurt a family and would never get in the way of a marriage. It was hard to believe that Benedict, who seemed otherwise perfect, appeared to have such different values. And as for that poor little boy, what would become of him if his father carried on in this vein? Benedict Redman was truly despicable and she hated him. To think she'd almost worn her mother's wedding wrap on a night out with him. She snorted and threw down the ephemeris.

An old, dog-eared piece of paper slid out and landed on the floor. Ashamed, she picked it up. It showed a large circle, with a smaller one inside it, creating a band that was divided into twelve and populated with the signs of the zodiac. The chart was also divided into twelve houses, ranging from the first house – the ascendant, or rising house – through to the twelfth house. Symbols for the planets were drawn at the appropriate degree in each sign and coloured lines linked the planets. These denoted the aspects: the angles made by the planets to one another.

Although it always caused some pain to look at this birth chart, it was her favourite, because her mother had cast it for her when she was born. Stella had seen all kinds of amazing charts in her time, ranging from heavily illustrated, hand-painted works of art through to crisp, modern charts churned out on computers. But this humble chart, drawn from scratch by her mother, was the most beautiful horoscope that she'd ever seen. Each glyph was neatly inked, and all the symbols for the angles between the planets were recorded faithfully in the table of aspects beneath the birth chart.

Her mother had lived long enough to pass on her knowledge about the beauty and the rhythm of the night sky, what each planet represented and what each sign signified. To make it easy for Stella to understand, her mother had explained that the planets were like actors in a play. The twelve zodiac signs they occupied were the costumes they wore. The houses from one to twelve that the planets resided in were the stage sets. And the aspects were the lines the actors spoke to each other.

Despite all these teachings, Stella had never seen her own birth chart. When she'd eventually started to go through the papers and books left by her parents, she found her chart, sealed inside a stiffened envelope. In turn, the envelope was tucked inside her mother's twentieth-century ephemeris, which was now hers. With the benefit of what her mother had taught her, combined with the power of the internet, Stella soon learned how to translate the birth chart and eventually worked out in her head what her heart had always known: that the horoscope in the stiffened envelope was hers.

Stella wondered why her mother hadn't interpreted the chart or left her some notes. All those years of teaching her daughter the basic tenets of astrology, and she'd never once shown her the chart she'd made. As Stella had grown older, and her understanding of astrology deepened, she realised that it was a fluid art, and believed that her mother had not wanted to project her own visions onto a life still forming. Her mother must have been tempted to look at the chart to see how her daughter's life would unfold, but without peeking into areas that were private. Stella's heart ached for her mother all the more for respecting her secrets and her as-yet unlived life. A mother's desire to know had been sacrificed to a daughter's right to develop at her own pace.

Carefully, she traced the chart with an index finger. She was born when the sun was in the water sign of Pisces, so that meant her 'sign' was Pisces in the popular parlance, and her moon was also in Pisces, right next to the sun. This conjunction of the two luminaries meant that she was doubly sensitive and compassionate, but not especially practical or realistic. The sun and moon also represented her mother and father, who had been together in life and together in death. Being placed in the fourth house, which represented home and roots, the restless moon mirrored the fact that Stella was never in one place long enough to consider it home.

The zodiac sign coming up over the horizon at the time she was born was Sagittarius, which gave her some fire, energy and optimism and made her appear more outgoing and adventurous than she actually was. Mars was conjunct her ascendant, but it was placed in the twelfth house, so this tempered her temper, meaning she struggled to be angry with the right person at the right time for the right reason, and as a consequence, often made her own life more difficult than it needed to be.

The symbols on the chart grew harder to see as her eyes blurred under a haze of tears. There they were in her birth chart. The two luminaries. The lights of her life. Sun and moon. Father and mother. Bound together in her horoscope and bound together in eternity. That was Stella's only comfort, that her parents had died together. In many ways, she wished she'd died too and stayed with her family, but it hadn't been her destiny, so she'd made a determined effort to live her life and to be glad of it. But she never held back from crying for her lost parents, trying to heal the wound that would never heal. People had always told her when she was a child that time healed all things, that in time the pain would leave her and she would forget. But it hadn't left her because she didn't want to forget. As painful as it was, she wanted to remember her parents and remain faithful to their memory.

Too upset to contemplate her birth chart any longer, she decided to go for a swim in the ladies pond on Hampstead Heath. If nothing else, spending some time in her own element would take her out of herself for a while.

She grabbed her swimming kit and set off along Abbey Road, past the red-brick and white plaster mansion flats, and continued through groves of vast white villas that made her feel as though she was running through a maze of gigantic wedding cakes. Onwards to Swiss Cottage and past shops and cinemas, through side streets, into pretty mews and out again into grand Victorian terraces. Up Parliament Hill, which was well named and made her thighs burn, and finally onto the last leg on the heath. Over the bridge across the mixed pond, she ran towards the ladies pond. Even though it was only just gone seven, the pond was already dotted with early-morning swimmers.

Nicely warmed up, Stella stripped to her red swimming costume, shoved her running things into a locker and ventured towards the pond. The air was warm, but the water would be colder, so she braced herself as she stepped down the ladder and submerged herself. Once she'd caught her breath, she swam out, her muscles unfurling and lengthening with every stroke. For once, she was glad of the in-built aloofness of Londoners and was pleased to be left in peace to swim and daydream. When her arms started to tire, she floated on her back and stared up at the blue sky, criss-crossed with trails from high-climbing planes taking people on holiday or to start new lives.

Outside her building, she bent over to catch her breath before opening the door. She'd not bothered with a shower after her swim as there was little point when she was running home. Instead, she'd towelled herself roughly, dragged on her clothes and shoved her wet hair into a hat to stop it snaking around her neck on the return journey. Ernie was busy watering the lobby plants and he raised his watering can on seeing her.

'Morning, Stella. Been swimming again?'

'I have, Ernie, but how did you possibly guess?'

'Got my sources,' he said, tapping the side of his nose. 'You been up the ponds again?'

'Only place to go.'

'Agreed. Used to go there regular as a young man. Not so keen on the cold water these days, mind. Not with my joints. Miss it something rotten, though.'

He winked and she grinned, not bothering to wait for the lift but trotting straight up the stairs to keep warm. Once inside the flat, she stripped and threw her wet things into the laundry basket then hopped into a welcome hot shower. After blow-drying her hair, she put on some jeans, pulled her pink jumper on over a white T-shirt and went to forage in the kitchen. Ravenous, she toasted a heap of sour-dough bread and smeared it with butter and honey while her coffee brewed, then she carried her breakfast out to the little table on the balcony and watched the world going by, returning occasional waves from the tourists hanging around outside the studio across the road.

During her swim, she'd reached the conclusion that it was definitely time that she returned to her old home in Durham. She chewed thoughtfully, filled with trepidation at the idea of raking over the cold embers of her family history. Her flat-sitting agreement generously allowed her a two-night break once a month, so she couldn't use being stuck in St John's Wood as an excuse not to go. Over coffee, she opened a hotel booking app and pondered the idea further. Apart from anything, it was hypocritical to counsel her clients to face up to their past in readiness for their Saturn return without taking a dose of her own medicine. It was now or never. Before she could change her mind, she booked a city-centre hotel room and rail tickets for the following weekend.

Now that she'd committed herself to going – financially, if not emotionally – she started getting cold feet. Although dreaming of nothing else for years, Stella was also afraid of not being able to cope with the pain of facing so many childhood memories in one go and wondered whether seven days was really long enough to allow her to acclimatise to the idea.

It had to be done though, if she was ever to feel whole and part of something bigger than herself. This journey to the past was a vital part of coming to terms with that past. Closure wasn't what she was looking for, because she never wanted to forget her family, but she wanted some sort of peace. She picked up her mug in both hands and shivered in spite of the warm coffee and her cosy jumper. This cold was coming from inside her and it would take more than hot drinks and warm clothing to dispel that.

She was jarred from her thoughts by her phone vibrating on the table. It was Benedict. Against her better judgement, she accepted the call. She had to get a grip. Even a double Pisces could surely show some backbone.

'Stella, I know you're angry with me, but I've no idea why. Please explain it to me. At least give me that. And then once we've ironed that out, I promise never to darken your door again, if that's what you want.'

Although she was still cross with Benedict, Stella was essentially fair-minded and found herself agreeing. If she was completely honest, she wanted to see just how he was going to wriggle out of this one. Knowing the truth would help her to put this troubling episode behind her, and besides, it might help her to figure out why the planets weren't chiming in quite the way she'd expect. All was definitely not well on the celestial front.

'Fair enough,' she said, 'although I don't see that it will help.'

'It's a bit difficult to talk about on the phone,' he said. 'Might we talk in person?'

This sounded like a ploy to win her round, and she started to stiffen.

'I can be in London in just over an hour, Stella. We can meet wherever you like – at your place or somewhere in town, if you prefer.'

'Don't you have work to do? And what about your family?'

'I've no lectures today, and my research can wait for a few hours. Daniel's grandparents have taken him ice-skating – worrying, I know – and I can easily get to London and back before he's due home.'

Stella had no client appointments until the evening, so it was no skin off her nose if he wanted to waste his time and money trying to talk her round.

'Fine, then. Abbey Road. NW8. St John's Wood to you. Straight opposite the recording studio.' She told him the name of the building and her flat number. 'I'll buzz you in, and if Ernie deems you worthy of admittance, he'll let you use the lift.'

She didn't bother to offer any directions, assuming that someone who knew his way around the universe could probably find his way around north-west London without too much trouble.

Chapter Five

When she heard Benedict's voice on her intercom, Stella buzzed him in without speaking, then stood in her doorway waiting for the lift to clank its way up the shaft.

'You'd better come in,' she said, when he emerged from the lift.

'Thank you,' he said, and followed her into the flat. 'Lovely place, Stella.'

'Agreed, though I can't take any credit as it's only on loan to me.'

It was a lovely flat. The oak floorboards were sanded and oiled so they were rich and warm, covered in part with a large rug in early autumnal shades of gold and green. The high waffle ceiling was matt white, as were the walls, which made the open-plan apartment fresh and clean. Heavy cream curtains framed both the bay window and the French doors. There was little furniture other than a small table, two wooden chairs and a sumptuous cream sofa that was very unforgiving of stains.

'Well, you agreed to hear me out, so shall we?' He hovered near the sofa until she indicated that he could sit down.

'I suppose you'll want tea?'

'Please,' he said, consulting his watch. 'Although coffee would be fine. It's still morning, just about.'

Stella went into the kitchen to make coffee, unable to believe that anyone had to check the time to decide whether to drink tea or coffee. And who even wore wristwatches these days? She whizzed some beans in the grinder and poured the ground coffee into the pot before sticking it on the hob. While the pot boiled, she clanked around with mugs to cover her nervousness. This was a very bad idea. Her visitor was even better looking than she'd remembered, and now he was here in her flat being all proper. She allowed herself a quick peek at him. He was standing looking out of the bay window, where the morning rays caught his hair, setting it alight so he was haloed in gold. Unfair. Even the sun was taking his side. He turned then, and caught her looking at him. Stella's heart thumped, but she managed to force out some words.

'Um, I forgot to ask how you like it. Coffee, that is. You know. Cream, sugar, that sort of thing.'

'On its own, please.'

Should have been obvious, really. Anyone so straight and upright wouldn't have any soft edges, so that would rule out cream and sugar. She paused before heaping her own cup with four sugars and a double portion of cream. She carried the coffee in along with a small plateful of shortbread that she'd made – guiltily – especially for this meeting, reasoning that she had to occupy her time somehow while she waited as it was impossible to concentrate on work and she couldn't settle into her book.

He took the tray from her and set it on the table. 'Well, these look too good to resist,' he said, helping himself. 'Home-made?'

She nodded and tried not to stare at him while he ate. Instead, she reminded herself that she only needed to hear what he had to say and then get rid of him. This had to end now. Or at least it had to end once he'd finished eating his third biscuit.

'You might as well say your piece,' she said. 'It must be good since you've travelled all this way.'

'I'm not so sure about good. It's just rather complicated, that's all.'

'Something told me it might be. Go on then, spill your guts.'

'Charmingly put.' He crossed his legs, revealing a couple of inches of leg above a striped sock.

'Any time today will be fine.' Stella forced herself to be hard.

He was reaching for a fourth biscuit, thought better of it and rubbed his ear instead.

'First and foremost, you seem to be under the impression that I'm married.'

'Oh, please. There's no impression about it, my friend. I even saw you being ticked off for talking to me the first time we met at Greenwich. And then that night at South Ken, your mate with all the loopy hair went out of his way to tell me as much.'

'Loopy hair?'

'Corduroy suit the colour of quinoa.'

'Oh,' he said, realisation dawning, 'you must mean Nigel. More colleague than friend. What did he say to you?'

'He more or less warned me off you. Saying Miranda wouldn't be happy.'

'Miranda wouldn't be happy?'

'Yes, the blonde woman from the observatory. Miranda, your wife.'

On hearing this, his eyebrows shot up. 'Well, Nigel's not wrong. Miranda probably won't be happy, but not because she's my wife. Miranda is my sister.'

'Your sister?' Oh, no. This was embarrassing to the power of ten, and what a nasty piece of work this Nigel had turned out to be.

'In fact, she's my twin sister. We're monozygotic twins.'

'Mono-zy-what-ic?'

'It just means we're identical because we're from the

same egg. Whereas fraternal twins are no more identical than any other pair of siblings – they've shared the womb, but nothing more. Sorry, Stella. I'm off into lecture mode. Bad habit of mine, I'm afraid.'

Looking into his pale-blue eyes, she could forgive this man any number of bad habits. She was fizzing inside. He wasn't married and Miranda was his sister. Result!

'Did you really not notice any resemblance?'

'None at all. You have similar colouring, but personality-wise, it's hard to believe that you two are even related, let alone twins. Sorry. I shouldn't be so rude about a member of your family.'

'My sister can appear quite frosty. It's the barrister in her, I imagine.'

Of course she was a barrister, but most importantly, a barrister who was a twin sister. Stella felt warmer towards Miranda already and passed the plate to Benedict, who took another biscuit.

'You might as well finish them off. There are loads left in the kitchen. Shall I pack them up and you can take them home for Daniel?'

'That's very kind. He does enjoy shortbread although he might have to fight me off.'

'No fighting necessary. I batch-baked, so you'll struggle to carry them all on the train.'

'The more the merrier. It's been a long time since we've had anything home-baked by anyone other than me.'

He looked wistful and she felt a catch in her throat. Now that he'd mentioned Daniel, she couldn't avoid the question lurking in the back of her mind.

'Benedict, may I ask you a question?'

He nodded, obviously knowing what was coming because he put his half-eaten biscuit down and looked at her.

'We've established that Miranda's your sister, and we're clear that Daniel's your son, right?'

'Er, yes. Right.'

'Well, he must have a mother. Sorry, I don't mean to intrude. It's just, you know...'

'I know.' He looked down at the floor between his feet. 'Daniel's mother – my wife, Anna.'

On hearing this, her heart sank. Whatever he said next was awful for Daniel. Stella wasn't sure she was ready to tread through someone else's pain, but she'd asked the question and would have to face whatever came by way of answer.

'Daniel's mother. My wife, Anna.' Benedict seemed to reach deep inside himself and stared into the middle distance as if looking into a different time. 'She died shortly after giving birth to Daniel. There were complications.'

'I'm so sorry, Benedict.' It was heartfelt. Stella could see the man before her crumpling. Perhaps he was back in that time, remembering his wife, and feeling the loss for himself and his baby boy. There was nothing more she could say, and they sat for a few moments in uneasy silence. When Benedict looked back at her, tears glazed his eyes.

'It was nearly seven years ago, but I still find it difficult to talk about. Do you mind if we change the subject?'

'Of course not. I'm sorry for putting you on the spot like that.'

'It's my own fault for not explaining sooner that I'm a widower and not a married man.'

He gave a rueful smile and Stella yearned to comfort him, but she was frozen. He was still in pain for his wife, and it would be wrong to touch him. She was ashamed now for her tantrummy behaviour. The poor man had done nothing wrong at all. Far from being an unfaithful husband looking for some extra-curricular activity, he'd been widowed many years ago, and it broke her heart that both he and his little boy had gone through so much tragedy. This was a different man to the assured professor he'd appeared to be at his lectures. It went some way to explaining why Daniel wasn't quite as boisterous or as cheeky as the average six-year-old.

By now, the coffee had gone cold. 'I'll make some tea,'

she said, for the sake of something to say. 'It's afternoon now. Just.'

When she came back, bearing a tray holding two cups and a teapot, Benedict had composed himself and took the tray from her. They drank their tea quietly while Stella kicked herself for storming off the other night instead of just asking for an explanation there and then. When he'd finished his tea, Benedict set down his empty cup, picked up the tray and headed for the kitchen, with Stella following behind.

'I have to get back for Daniel, but how would you feel about coming to spend some time with us? You could come for a weekend if you like and suffer some of my home-baking. Fair exchange being no robbery and all that.'

This was a very welcome invitation, but Stella had to turn it down and explained that she'd only just booked train tickets to go north to visit her old family home in Durham. She avoided any mention of her parents. There was enough death in the room for one day. Because her flat-sitting contract only allowed her one weekend away per month, it would be ages before she could visit Benedict.

'Say hi to Daniel for me.' She handed him a greaseproof paper package, neatly tied. 'Ask him what his favourites are, and I'll make some before I see you next time.'

'You're too kind, Stella. He'll enjoy these, thank you. Well, I must be off. Good luck in Durham.'

She set him to the door and they stood by the lift, with the ghost of his wife still in the air. When the lift dinged, Benedict stuck out his hand and Stella, hiding her disappointment, shook it.

Once he was away in the lift, Stella ran to the balcony and watched for him coming out of her building and walking down the street. Even though it was warm, he pulled his brown suede jacket around him before digging his phone from his pocket, frowning over it, then looking up at the street signs. She laughed as he disappeared around the corner. So, the man who was at home in the universe was entirely lost in the streets of London.

She hugged herself, cursing her flat-sitting contract. At the time of signing, she'd been impressed at the owner's generosity – this was a lovely flat in a desirable area, so the owner would have probably got any number of takers, even if they'd had to spend every single night here. But now, only being allowed out for one weekend a month felt like being locked in a prison cell – albeit a rather luxurious one.

In the morning, Stella woke up feeling under the weather, and her head felt too thick to do the three client readings booked in for later that afternoon. She hated letting people down, so she ran herself a hot bath in the hope it would get rid of her sniffles and leave her well enough to work.

From the bathroom cabinet, she took a wooden box containing six dark glass bottles, each an inch high. First, she checked the labels, then added six drops from the bottle of lavender, three from the rosemary and two from the peppermint. This was one of her mother's many recipes, and until medical science found a cure for the common cold, Stella would also rely on the old ways. She pinned up her hair and breathed deeply as she lowered herself into the tub, where the fragrant steam started to clear her head and the hot water drew the aches out of her long bones.

Hopefully, she'd just caught a chill from swimming in pond water or running home with wet hair and wasn't coming down with Covid. She'd had it once and was in no hurry to repeat that particular experience. More likely, the emotional turmoil of the last couple of days had affected her. While she was pleased to have resolved things with Benedict, it was difficult dealing with the fact that he was free only because his wife had died tragically. Her heart went out to him. It must have been very hard facing such pain as he brought up his little boy alone. And how hard it must have been for Daniel. At least Stella had known her parents before losing them and she had twelve years of happy memories. Poor kid didn't even have those.

———

Later that evening, after she'd finished her client readings, Stella was in her pyjamas, sipping a hot brew of lemon, garlic and honey when her phone rang.

'Hello, Benedict. Is everything all right?'

'Yes, yes it is. I felt bad for dashing off without making firm arrangements to see you again.'

'No worries, I know you had a train to catch. Did you make it back in time?'

'Yes, thank you, and thank you also for the biscuits. Daniel adores them. I'm going to struggle to fob him off with the shop-bought kind from now on.'

'You don't need to, I can send some up for him. It's good to have an appreciative audience for a change.'

'Well, I was wondering… Your flat-sitting contract. Does it stipulate one weekend off per calendar month, or is it once every four weeks?'

Odd question. 'Once per calendar month.'

'Excellent news. Now, you're away this weekend, and I'm out of the country the following weekend, but how do you feel about coming to see us the weekend after that? It will be a new calendar month, I'm reliably informed, so you have no excuse.'

He was right. Her contract stated one weekend every calendar month, so there was no need to wait for ages. Even so, two-and-a-half weeks might as well be two-and-a-half years.

'I'd like that.' *I'd love that* was what she really meant, but love was a dangerous word to bandy about. 'Just tell me where and when.'

'I'll give it some thought and drop you a line. So you're all set for Durham this weekend, then?'

'Yes, all set.' By dropping her a line, did he mean he was going to send something by snail mail? Curious behaviour, but it would be nice to get an actual letter, she supposed.

'Which train are you getting?'

'The nine-thirty from King's Cross on Saturday morning, which should get me there for not too long after midday.'

'I hope you have a wonderful time.'

This was highly unlikely, but Benedict wasn't to know that. She'd have to tell him about her parents some time, but not just now.

They chatted for a minute or two more and then rang off. It was good that they'd arranged to meet again, even if it was over a fortnight away, but that couldn't be helped. Benedict had a busy work schedule, plus he had Daniel, and she wasn't exactly just around the corner either. She should have invited them to Durham, but that felt like too big an imposition.

Still, the time would pass. She'd have an early night and hopefully shake off whatever was ailing her. The next few days would fill up with packing and organising, and the weekend in Durham would fly over. Then there'd only be eleven days to go until she saw Benedict again. Eleven days. It felt like a long time.

Chapter Six

At nine on Saturday morning, Stella was inside King's Cross station, standing beneath a white steel tree whose geometric branches soared to the roof and created a giant canopy above the concourse. She'd bought the largest cup of coffee the station had to offer and was busy scrutinising the departures screen. At nine-fifteen, the train started boarding and she wandered down the platform, looking for her carriage. Her reservation was at a table of four, where she settled into her window seat and set out her book, coffee, phone and earbuds. Although the train was filling up, her table remained empty. When the tannoy started booming overhead, she plugged in her earbuds, hoping to drown it out with music.

Three-quarters of an hour later, when the train stopped at Peterborough, there was some jostling as her table started to fill. Not in the right frame of mind to chat with strangers, she buried her nose in her book. By the time she'd pretended to read two pages, the train started to shunt out of the station, and Stella was once again on her way to make peace with her past. Her mind was racing too much to concentrate and there was no way she could pretend to read all the way to Durham when it was still almost two hours away. Instead, she'd leave her earbuds in and gaze out of the window. Providing she didn't make eye contact with anyone at her table, she'd be fine. Her plan was ruined when she closed her book and caught sight of a little boy sitting opposite with his finger over his lips, eyes dancing with laughter. Amazed, she looked to the boy's right. There sat his father in a similar state of disrepair.

'Daniel? Benedict? What the… I mean, what on earth?'

'Sorry, Stella. I hope you don't mind us gate-crashing your trip. Only, we couldn't resist.'

'Far from it,' she said. 'It's lovely to see you. But what brought you?'

'Two-and-a-half weeks felt like two weeks too long. I wanted to see you again and thought you might be glad of the company. If it's a bother, we can hop off at Grantham.'

'You'll do no such thing. It's no bother at all and I'm glad to see you.' She winked at Daniel. 'Both of you.'

And she was glad. When she'd looked up and saw them, it had taken a moment to sink in properly. To think that Benedict had given up his time, to say nothing of his money – last-minute train tickets and hotel rooms didn't exactly come cheap – to travel all this way with her. It had to be a good sign, and Stella didn't even need to check the planets to work that one out.

'So,' said Benedict, 'have you had breakfast yet?'

'No, I wasn't hungry first thing and planned to grab a sarnie when the trolley comes by.'

'We can do a bit better than a trolley sandwich. Let's see if the dining car's on and get ourselves something more substantial. Come on. My treat and no arguments.'

They made their way down the train to the dining car, which was laid out with white linen and silver cutlery, crockery and glasses. They sat down and soon found themselves tucking into a full English breakfast. Benedict cut Daniel's toast into soldiers so he could dip them in the yolk of his fried egg. Stella was surprised to see such a little boy manage to eat so much.

'You're a good eater, aren't you, Daniel?'

'Mmff,' replied Daniel through a mouthful of eggy toast.

'It's his rocket-fuel.' Benedict tickled his son's neck. 'You need it to fly to the moon and back each day, don't you?'

Daniel gulped some milk, grinned happily and wiped the resulting creamy moustache on his sleeve. His father side-eyed him and produced a napkin.

'Dragged up, I'm afraid.'

Daniel took the napkin and wiped his already clean mouth on it.

'Say, Daniel,' said Stella, 'did you eat all the biscuits I sent you?'

'Yes, they were delish. Will you make me some more?'

'That's a very bold request, son. Please try to remember that it's not polite to ask for presents.'

'Sorry, Daddy. Sorry, Stella.'

'It's all right, Daniel. I'm more than happy to make some more. What's your favourite kind?'

Daniel poked a finger in his chin and stared up at the ceiling for some time.

'Emmmmm... I like chocolate and cherry and broccoli best.'

'Chocolate and cherry, I get, but broccoli? In a biscuit? Are you sure about that?'

'Yes. I love broccoli. It's my favourite.'

'Chocolate, cherry and broccoli it is. Let me see what I can do.'

Stella typed a note into her phone, raising a brow at Benedict for confirmation.

'Broccoli is a firm favourite in our house, although I'm not too sure I'd personally want to eat it in a biscuit.'

Benedict paid the bill and the waiter was in the process of clearing the table when Daniel asked his father (and the rest of the carriage) in a stage whisper to take him for a wee.

'Come on then, son. Stella, shall we see you back at our table?'

On returning to their seats, Benedict gave his son a dinosaur colouring book. With a crayon firmly clenched in one hand, and his tongue firmly poked out of the corner of his mouth to aid concentration, Daniel set about colouring in a stegosaurus.

'I still can't believe you've both come along,' said Stella. 'Where are you going to stay?'

'Same place as you, I hope.'

'I didn't tell you where I'm staying.'

'No, but I took a guess.'

'Did you? You're remarkably sure of yourself for someone who had to use satnav to find his way back to the same Tube station he'd arrived at barely an hour earlier.'

'You saw me! I'm dreadful with directions. Unless I've done the trip at least a dozen times, it doesn't sink in, and sometimes not even then.'

'Yet you can find your way around the universe with perfect ease.'

'It's both embarrassing and illogical. You'd think the same part of the brain would deal with both sets of directions, but it doesn't compute when my feet are on the ground for some reason.'

He took out his phone and tapped it a few times before showing Stella the screen. It turned out that he was a good guesser and had booked the same hotel. After a bit of interrogation, he confessed to choosing the first hotel that came up on the booking app, which is exactly what Stella had done.

Daniel put down his colouring book and looked out of the window. 'Are we nearly there yet, Daddy?'

'Yes, son. This is York, so we have less than an hour, but that should be more than long enough for you to do a new picture.'

'Great, I'm going to do a brontosaurus next.'

While he continued colouring in, Stella took the opportunity to explain to Benedict the real reason for her journey to Durham. He said nothing but took her hands between his own and looked at her with so much compassion that she was in danger of crying and had to turn away. She spent the rest of the journey staring out of the window, watching the verdant countryside scrolling past, dotted with occasional farms and divided by neat hedgerows and stone walls. When they passed Darlington, Benedict helped Daniel to tidy away his colouring things and gathered their belongings.

'It's best to be standing near the door before we pull in,' said Stella, 'then you can enjoy the best view of the castle and the cathedral instead of rushing about collecting luggage.' That much at least she remembered from trips with her parents.

As the train slowed down and pulled across the high viaduct into Durham station, Stella stared down on higgledy-piggledy terraces of houses, their roofs far below. Dominating the skyline was a green hill, crowned with two magnificent sandstone buildings.

She sighed. 'I'd forgotten how beautiful home is. Look at the castle and cathedral, Daniel. They're almost a thousand years old.'

The boy smiled up at his father. 'Is that nearly as old as you, Daddy?'

Benedict laughed and ruffled his son's hair. 'I'm a little bit younger than that, you cheeky so-and-so.'

'Perhaps we could go up there,' she suggested. 'What do you think, Daniel? Would you like to climb the cathedral tower? There are over three-hundred steps – I used to count them up and down every time I went as a little girl. From the top, you can see across the whole county.'

'Ooh! Can we, Daddy?'

After helping his son down from the train and holding the train door for Stella, Benedict promised his son that they could go up the tower as soon as they'd checked in to the hotel.

Daniel looked up and down the platform. 'Daddy, this is just like my train set at home, isn't it?'

Benedict examined the quaint station with its two short platforms, its slate and glass canopies and the little waiting room and was forced to agree that it bore an uncanny resemblance. Outside the station was a queue of white taxis waiting, and an even longer queue of people waiting to get into them.

'What do you want to do, Stella? Walk or taxi?'

'I could do with the walk after sitting down for so long. How about it, Daniel?'

The boy nodded and hopped up and down, holding onto his father's hand, and the three of them set off down the steep hill to walk through Durham.

The walk took them just over fifteen minutes and they soon found their hotel, which was situated on the banks of the River Wear, close to the cathedral and castle. Stella unpacked and sat on the comfortable bed to survey her room. It managed to be both spacious and cosy at the same time, and she was pleased to see there was a bath as well as a shower. Other than the birdsong filtering through her open window, she could hear nothing. From the window, the cathedral was visible and she wondered how it would feel venturing up the tower without her parents. Her thoughts were interrupted by a gentle rap on the door.

'Stelllaaaarrrrr, it's uu-uu-ss.'

'Hello us. Come on in – it's open.'

Daniel bounded in and gave the room a thorough examination.

'Are you sad because you've only got one room?' He knelt on the ottoman and peered out of the window. 'Me and daddy have got a bedroom each and a bathroom and another room with a funny little sofa in it and we can see the river as well. I've got a surprise for you. It's about the river but you have to guess what it is.'

'Really? Then I'll need to put my thinking cap on.'

'Your thinking cap? Where is it?' asked the eager boy. 'Is it in the wardrobe?'

Trying not to smile at him taking her so literally, Stella made a half-hearted search of her wardrobe before turning back with a sad expression on her face.

'It's not there. I must have left my thinking cap in London.'

'Well then you'll never guess, will she, Daddy?'

Benedict concurred that Stella was unlikely to guess what the secret was, so she'd have to remain in suspense until it was revealed.

Stella took them into a little nook that contained what must surely be the tiniest teashop in England. As they were still stuffed from breakfast, they opted to make do with a snack for the time being and have a proper meal later. They ordered a large pot of tea (it being afternoon) and a plateful of scones, with crocks of strawberry jam and clotted cream on the side. Within minutes, Daniel was smothered in a bit of everything he'd just eaten.

Benedict rubbed his son's smudged cheek with his handkerchief. 'Daniel, you look as if you've been coated in jam and rolled in breadcrumbs.'

Stella laughed. 'Come on, claggy bairn, it's time to tell me that secret of yours.'

'What's a claggy bairn?' asked Daniel.

'A sticky child – or in your case, a very sticky child.'

Together, they wended their way up cobbled streets and squeezed down secret vennels – which Stella remembered as clearly as if she'd never left – and soon found themselves on the river. Benedict whispered in his son's ear and Daniel skipped between the two adults.

'We're going to have the surprise now, Stella.'

'I love surprises,' she said, wiggling her eyebrows.

Daniel clutched her hand and whispered. 'Me too and I love going on boats best of all.'

Stella tried hard not to laugh and was impressed that the boy had managed to keep the secret to himself for as long as he had. At the boathouse, she was given the choice of boarding a large double-decker river cruiser, or being rowed in a small wooden boat. She couldn't make up her mind and delegated the decision to the youngest member of the party, who opted for the DIY voyage.

Benedict shepherded them into their chosen vessel and rowed them along the River Wear. The broad waterway flowed around the peninsula – where the castle and cathedral perched high above them – its wide loop acting as a natural moat. In the hands of an expert rower, Stella and Daniel lay back, lulled by the gentle motion of the boat, and gazed up at the precipitous, tree-clad riverbanks while they were rowed from bridge to bridge.

All around and above them, the trees were dark green and Stella trailed a hand in the cool, clear water. The air was soft and fresh, and not at all like the thicker vintage served up in London. So this was home. The small city where she'd been born and had left barely a dozen years later, leaving her with no more than memories. Why had she shied away from coming back for all these years when it was the only place she could truly call home? It hadn't hurt nearly as much as feared and she relished the quiet peace washing over her. Or at least she did until Daniel tired of resting and insisted on taking an oar for a turn at rowing. Father and son spent two hilarious minutes going round in circles, much to the little boy's consternation. Benedict eventually showed mercy and eased up on his side so they went in a straight-ish line back to the boathouse.

Once they'd recovered their land legs, they climbed up the winding cobbled streets to Palace Green, which separated the magnificent eleventh-century Norman cathedral and castle. They crossed the green and stood outside the cathedral door, pausing to admire the sanctuary ring. Stella explained how the knocker was made of bronze and that it most likely weighed more than the little boy. Benedict lifted Daniel up for a better look.

'It's a monster!' exclaimed the child.

'That's right,' said Stella, 'but it's a good monster designed to scare away evil.'

She told him the same story her father used to tell her on visits to the cathedral: that the monster was known as a hellmouth, which had eaten away so much of an unfortunate man that only his legs dangled from its jaws. To make matters worse, a two-headed snake gnawed on the man's feet. Long, long ago, anyone accused of a crime could claim sanctuary at the cathedral. All they had to do was seize the knocker and the monks would take them under their protection for forty days.

The little boy's eyes were round with wonder as he stretched out tentative fingers to seize the curved snake. Stella didn't spoil the magic by telling him the sanctuary ring was only a replica and that the real knocker was tucked away in the museum nowadays. She placed her own hand next to Daniel's. Benedict caught her eye and added his hand to the ring. They stayed like that for a moment until Stella broke the spell.

'Time for a selfie, eh? What do you reckon?'

Obligingly, the Redmans scrunched up close and she held her phone at arm's length, doing her best to get all three of them and the hellmouth into the picture.

Inside the vast cathedral, they walked in wonder, gazing up past the high galleries and into the ceiling vaults. Just before the entrance to the central tower, they stopped in front of an enormous golden clock and Stella pointed up at three small dials above the clock face, one of which showed the phases of the moon. The clock was so tall that Daniel couldn't see and his father had to hoist him onto his shoulders for a better look. Beneath the clock was a painting and Stella couldn't resist telling the boy that it was really a pair of secret doors that opened for the choir to enter during services.

After admiring the clock, they bought tickets and entered the tower, counting each of the three-hundred-and-twenty-five steps that spiralled round and round the twisting staircase. At the top of the stairs, they walked out onto the roof where they stood over two-hundred feet in the air with the wind blowing against their faces. All around them were rolling hills and vales, dark forests and silver rivers. After they'd traversed the roof and enjoyed the dizzying view from all four sides of the tower, they carefully made their way back down.

Before leaving the cathedral, they paused to make a donation, sign the visitors' book and light some candles. Benedict allowed Daniel to light the spill from the votive candle, covering the boy's hand with his own to steady him as he touched the flame to the wick of the tealight. Once all three candles were lit, they breathed in the smell of melting candlewax and stood in silent meditation, praying for their loved ones until Daniel demanded to know why Stella had two candles while he had to share one with his father.

Benedict rubbed his hair and picked him up. 'Because, darling boy, we've lit one candle for your mother and Stella has lit one each for her mother and her father.'

The little boy nodded, taking this in. 'Stella, are your mummy and daddy in heaven the same as my mummy?'

Staring at his innocent little eyes reflecting the flickering flames, it was all she could do not to cry, so she gently took his hand and nodded at him.

'They are, Daniel. They are.' At least, she hoped they were.

Chapter Seven

After the cathedral visit, the three of them dined at a restaurant down by the river. On the walk back to their hotel afterwards, Benedict paused to catch his breath and clutched his side.

'I've got a stitch. Knew I shouldn't have helped Stella to finish her sticky toffee pudding...'

'But Daddy, you didn't help Stella at all. You just scoffed the lot!'

Benedict kissed his censorious son and the little boy scampered the last few yards to the hotel, leaving the two adults to catch up.

'I hope you don't mind spending your evening in our room. I thought Daniel might have lasted past seven o'clock, but he's absolutely shattered, despite all appearances to the contrary.'

'It's fine by me. I'm not much of a one for night-life to be honest.'

Daniel raced upstairs, dragging Stella by the hand, and showed her round what turned out to be more of a suite than a room, with two bedrooms, a bathroom and a sitting area, complete with a small chaise longue.

'All that was left at the last-minute,' said Benedict. 'Take a seat. I ordered a bottle of red earlier and thought that once his nibs falls asleep, we could have a glass and watch a film. Do you want to pick something while I read a bedtime story?'

'No problem, but if you hate it, then don't blame me.'

'I'm willing to take my chances. Right, sir, let's get you ready for bed.'

With that, he picked his son up by a leg and an arm and carried him off to the en suite where there was a good deal of giggling and not very much toothbrushing by the sound of things. Daniel gambolled back into the room wearing some blue tartan pyjamas and bounced into bed singing a song that Stella didn't recognise. There's a child who won't be sleeping anytime soon, she thought to herself as she waved goodnight. During story time, she busied herself looking for a film to watch that they'd both enjoy. Nothing depressing, but also nothing with love, sex or romance, which would be mortifying to watch.

Benedict returned from tucking Daniel into bed and put the book down on a side table.

'Well, that was easy,' said Stella.

'It's not normally, believe you me. He was sound asleep before I'd managed to read three pages. I'd expected more of a battle but I think the big dinner did for him.'

'I'm almost out for the count myself and probably won't need to eat again until Christmas. Now, on the film front, I've narrowed it down to a documentary about a donkey sanctuary – which I promise is more uplifting than it sounds – or a film about a pilgrimage across Europe where the pilgrims have to walk on their knees. As an added bonus, that one has subtitles.'

'Hmm, maybe we'll skip the box in that case.'

Benedict held up a bottle of red wine and when Stella nodded, he opened it and poured them a glass each. He joined her on the chaise, which was snug to say the least. The wine was so perfectly close to blood temperature that she felt she was inhaling it rather than drinking it. She started to melt, but wasn't sure whether that was due to the wine or the company. Stella was suddenly conscious of Benedict sitting close to her – so close that she could feel the warmth from his body, and close enough to breathe in something reminiscent of nutmeg or sandalwood. She didn't trust herself with another glass of wine inside her and decided not to drink any more. It was hard thinking of something to say and she contemplated putting on the donkey sanctuary documentary to cover the awkward silence but was spared by Daniel announcing that he needed another wee.

'Sorry, Stella. I'll just get him sorted. That last milkshake might have been a bad idea. Help yourself to more wine if you like.'

She shook her head. 'Another glass will knock me out. I'm a one-glass limit as a rule, and I already had a glass with dinner.'

While Benedict was otherwise occupied, she ran through her plans for the following day. First, an early morning walk to her old home. Her parents had rented an attic flat in a Victorian townhouse perched on a hill near the railway station. It had a long garden running down to the road behind it, but that belonged to the people who owned the house and her family were never allowed to use it, so her parents used to take her to the park across the road. Short of knocking on the door, there was no way of knowing whether the house was still owned by the same people, but she guessed that anyone who wouldn't allow a little girl to play in a huge garden they never used probably wouldn't welcome her inside years later to relive her childhood. Instead, she'd content herself with standing outside the house to see what she could remember, and she'd lay some flowers.

She was glad that Benedict and Daniel had come along, and it had made a difficult journey much easier, but she needed to do this final part by herself. All day, she'd been so busy that there'd not been time to think or reflect. Now, tired and mellowed by the wine, she started to feel a bit raw, thinking about her mother and father. It had hit her today in the cathedral, when they'd stopped and lit candles and wrote prayers for their loved ones. Seeing all those other candles burning had brought home to her the certain knowledge that loss was inevitable: to love someone was to risk losing them.

These feelings threatened to overwhelm her. The wine had been a bad idea on top of returning to her family's birthplace and in close company with this man and his son who shared such a similar wound. She closed her eyes to hold back the tears that were threatening to fall.

Stella was awakened by a ray of sun coming through the heavy curtains, so she pulled the covers over her face. She felt thick-headed and anxious, probably due to the wine from the night before. What was odd though, was that she couldn't remember returning to her room. Suddenly, a small form landed on her and knocked the wind out of her.

'Mmmppphhh,' was all she managed to say.

The small form pulled back the blankets and stared at her.

'Stella?'

'Daniel?' How did you get in here?' If she was going to sleep in hotel rooms without bothering to look her door, she'd better think about becoming teetotal.

'I was already in here. Why are you in Daddy's bed, Stella? Where's my daddy?'

'Umm, that's a good question, and I hope to have an answer for you any minute now.'

Oh, surely not, and especially not with Daniel barely ten feet away. She pulled the blankets closer to her, wondering where Benedict was. Obviously, he couldn't bear to see her this morning and had scarpered. No wonder she'd woken up feeling anxious. This was bad. While she was agonising,

Benedict entered the room, carrying a cup of coffee and a glass of milk.

'Good morning, sleepyheads. Thought I'd pop down and fetch you both a drink.'

He passed the milk to Daniel, who gulped it happily, and held out the cup of coffee to her. Stella froze. How could she take the cup from him and remain decent? Had he no consideration when his little boy was right next to the bed? This was too embarrassing for words, and Benedict seemed to be enjoying himself at her expense.

'If you have a headache,' he said with a smirk, 'I can go and get you something for it.'

Now that she was wide awake, Stella didn't have a thick head any more but was glad of the excuse to get rid of the Redmans while she made herself decent and nipped to the loo.

'That would be good, thanks. And maybe you could take you-know-who with you.'

'Back in a tick. Come on, Dan Dan, give me a hand.'

As father and son left the room, Stella took her chance and crawled out of bed, only then realising she'd worried unnecessarily about her modesty. She was still fully dressed, apart from her trainers, which were placed neatly at the side of the bed. What had been going on? In the bathroom, she smoothed her hair and splashed her face, before returning to find Benedict waving a small packet.

'Hotel reception – very helpful people. We're going to have breakfast downstairs before we go and explore the castle, if you'd care to join us.'

'Thanks, but not for me. After a nice long shower in my own room, I'll be straight out for the morning, but don't let me stop you two.'

'Fair enough. How about you, Daniel?'

'Not yet, Daddy. I need to watch two cartoons.'

'I see. Well, two cartoons it is and then we'll go and eat.'

While Daniel guffawed at the antics of colourful monsters on the small screen, Benedict owned up that Stella had nodded off and he hadn't the heart to wake her so he'd picked her up and put her in his bed, fully clothed.

'I did take your shoes off or you'd have had a very uncomfortable night. Your trainers took quite a bit of unknotting, I must say. Triple knots.'

Stella looked at him over her coffee. 'And where did you sleep?'

One eyebrow twitched and there was a ghost of a smile.

'I spent the night on the chaise longue.'

'On the chaise short, more like. It's barely long enough for two people to sit on so how did you manage to lie on it?'

'I didn't,' he said. 'My feet and most of my legs spent the night on the floor.'

'You should have woken me up and turfed me out.'

'It's not a problem. Plus you'd have missed Daniel's wake-up call.'

'Oh, the full-on aerial assault. Yes, wouldn't have missed that for the world.'

It was early and most of the shops were shut so the streets were still quiet and Stella enjoyed the peaceful morning air as she walked around the city in search of flowers. As it was Sunday, it didn't look like anywhere was going to open, but she found a mini supermarket with a small selection of cut flowers. Armed with pink, yellow and white roses, she set off to find her old home. Her only home, really.

She strolled past the front gate as casually as she could and glanced into the garden. The door was still painted a dull red and the curtains in the owner's living room were the same brown velvet that she recalled from her childhood. In all likelihood, it hadn't changed hands, and as much as she would have loved to set foot in her old home, she really couldn't face asking and being turned down. Instead, she walked down the terrace, back the way she'd come, remembering all the happy comings and goings from this house over the years, when she'd never once suspected what lay in her family's future. Often, she'd wondered whether her mother had foreseen the car crash in her own chart. She suspected not, or they wouldn't have moved so far away from home where their young daughter knew not a soul.

At the bottom of the terrace, Stella turned left and made her way around to the back garden. The terraced houses were built into a steep hill, with long gardens tumbling down from them. Because they were built into the hill, from the front, they appeared only two or three storeys high, but from the back, many of the houses had five or six storeys. Most of the sprawling gardens were overgrown with trees and shrubs so at least she wouldn't be easily observed from the house. She approached the back gate and stood for some time, staring up the sloping garden to the house looming over her with its grand bay windows. It was just possible to make out the garret flat that had been her home. Always, she'd wondered what might have happened if her family had never left and moved to Wiltshire. Perhaps her parents would still be there now, boiling strange herbs for tea, sewing their own clothes and stargazing. But they had moved, and they had died, and nothing she could do, say or think would ever change that.

When she was a girl, no one had ever used these back gates due to the steep access, so she doubted the people living there would notice her flowers tied to the gatepost and they'd hopefully stay there for a while. She wound a piece of ribbon round and round the stone gatepost, fastening the roses securely. Then, her breathing ragged, she kissed her fingertips and pressed them to the stone, thinking about her parents and giving thanks for the years they'd had together and grieving for the years they'd lost. Weighed down by a heavy sense of loss, she said goodbye to her parents, wishing that she didn't have to lose them all over again.

Chapter Eight

The train ride to London was uneventful. Daniel, who was tired out from a weekend of walking, rowing and fresh air, spent most of the journey colouring in, and before they reached York, he'd fallen asleep. Stella and Benedict talked in hushed tones until they neared Peterborough station, where Benedict gathered their things, leaned over the table and took Stella's hand.

'Thank you for letting us share your trip to Durham. I hope we weren't too much of an imposition?'

'Not at all, and I was really glad of the company.'

'I'll see you in a fortnight. Less than a fortnight.'

With that, Benedict scooped up his sleeping son and carried him to the door as the train started to slow. Pressing her face to the window, Stella watched him striding down the platform. He couldn't wave as his arms were full, but he turned and smiled, leaving her with the same melting feeling she'd had in the hotel room the previous night. Maybe it hadn't just been the wine, after all.

Back in her London flat, Stella put the kettle on to boil and changed into her pyjamas. She brewed a cup of chamomile tea, drizzled in some honey and curled up on the sofa to reflect on her weekend. For so many years, she'd put off a trip home, never really feeling that she could face it, but she'd done it, at last. She'd never truly come to terms with losing her parents, but it had calmed her soul lighting candles at the cathedral and laying flowers outside her old home. Her memories of the city were happy ones and it had been good to share her childhood haunts with Benedict and his son. It wouldn't have felt right had anyone else been there – not that she had anyone else to invite – but their shared sorrow created a sense of solidarity between them, so their presence was a comfort, rather than a burden.

That wasn't something she could say about many people in her life. She'd had friends over the years, and occasional boyfriends, but no one that had ever stuck because she was a permanently moving target. That was mostly deliberate – if she didn't stay still long enough, she couldn't form attachments to anyone and then she couldn't be hurt when they invariably left her. It was an ingrained pattern by now, and she was aware that it wasn't a healthy way to live: relying on no one and allowing no one to rely on her. A twenty-something orphan, independent to the point of being a hermit, and now this widowed astronomy professor and his six-year-old son had entered her life.

She was drawn to Benedict even though it was a terrible idea. The man was clearly still in mourning for his wife, then there was his son to think of, and Stella would be gone from London before too long. She was due to stay in Canada for six months and had been looking forwards to that for ages but was now starting to feel less certain. If she gave enough notice, she could ditch that assignment and needn't feel too guilty because it was a golden opportunity and there'd be a waiting list of people ready to take it on, so she'd hardly lose any reputation points, let alone risk being levelled down for it.

A few days later, Stella received a letter, which she almost ignored. Post addressed to her was a rarity and she was used to piling up mail for the owner. But something about the large, shaky letters caught her eye and she smiled when she saw her name spelt with a back-to-front 'S'. She took the envelope to the kitchen to open while she made some coffee.

Inside the envelope was a piece of paper, folded inexpertly into four, illustrated with a castle and three people: two tall and one small. The small person in the middle was Daniel, grinning up at the two big people. The Stella person was half the height of the Benedict person and several times wider, but she had lovely curly hair, a big smile and thick, spidery eyelashes. Benedict was very tall, very thin and wearing an astronaut suit. Stella laughed and turned the page over. On the back was a picture of a wobbly birthday cake bearing seven candles, with Daniel's name underneath followed by seven kisses. There was also a smaller piece of paper, neatly written, with an Oxford address in the top right-hand corner.

Dear Stella,

Thank you for allowing us to join you on your trip to Durham. We had a lovely time and wanted to say thank you. It's Daniel's birthday the weekend after next. If you're able to come, I could pick you up from Oxford station on Friday afternoon and drop you back there on Sunday evening. We do hope you can come as Daniel is itching to introduce you to his teddy.

Yours sincerely, Benedict and Daniel

Yours sincerely? It had been going so well until the formal sign-off, which was only marginally better than *Yours faithfully* or *Kind regards* (which in Stella's experience no one ever meant kindly). Evidently, she'd misread things. Talk about being friend-zoned. Well, that might not be a bad thing – no commitment, no messy feelings and easy to leave behind when it was time to move on. It looked like Canada was still on the cards after all. She picked up her phone to text but decided it would be better to reply in kind. In her satchel, she had some good-quality paper and coloured ink that she used for clients who wanted hand-drawn birth charts. Carefully folding a sheet of paper into four, she chewed her pen for a second or two before drawing a happy lion with a fluffy mane, complete with spectacles and dimples. Inside the card she drew the symbol for Leo and wrote:

Dear Daniel,
    I would love to come to your birthday party and can't wait to meet your teddy bear.
    Lots of love from Stella x x x x x x x

On a second piece of paper, she wrote to inform Benedict of her arrival time, mirroring his formal *Yours sincerely*. She put each piece of paper into separate envelopes and addressed them. It would have been easier and cheaper to put them both in the same envelope, but it was exciting for kids to get their own post.

Every year, Stella's parents had posted her cards to her so they'd arrive on the morning of her birthday. In the children's home, she'd always felt a prick of disappointment when she came downstairs and saw her cards neatly stacked behind the mantel clock. It was ungrateful of her when the staff and other kids had been kind enough to give her cards, but deep down, she knew it was her parents that she was missing and not the fact that they mailed her cards.

When she came back from the postbox, Stella sat down to cast a horoscope for Daniel. She had a good idea of his place and time of birth from little things Benedict had said, and now she knew the exact date. She would draw a special chart illustrated with lions, and when she got to Oxford, she'd spend some time telling the little boy about the planets' different personalities the same way her mother had taught her when she was small. The sun was the father, the moon was the mother, Mars the warrior, Venus the maiden,

Mercury the messenger, Jupiter the kindly teacher, and Saturn keeping watch over all as Old Father Time, until the arrival of Uranus the rebel, Neptune the magician and Pluto the destroyer. It might be fun for him to learn about another side to the planets, apart from just their physical qualities.

She'd buy him a present as well, but what to get? Just like his father, he was interested in space and rockets, so he might like an orrery: a small working model of the solar system, complete with moving planets. She looked online for a stockist and was pleased to find that one of the big museums near South Kensington had a couple in their shop. She could order it online but going to the museum would get her out of the house for a couple of hours and she could examine it in person

As she was about to set off to South Ken, Stella was struck by a thought: an orrery was really nothing more than educational apparatus disguised as a toy. Daniel was the son of a professor, he had no mother and he'd been brought up in a university town. Stella was willing to bet that all the gifts Daniel had ever been given would be educational apparatus disguised as toys, so instead of the museum shop, she headed for Regent Street to visit Hamleys.

The seven-storey toyshop was such a wonderful place that she regretted not bringing the boy himself to choose his own present, but that would mean turning up for his party empty-handed, so she'd do her best to choose for him. The shop floors were festooned with a bewildering array of toys: dolls, teddies, cars, trucks, trains, wooden toys, electronic toys, building toys, soft toys and noisy toys. There was far too much choice and it was hard to know where to begin as she knew no children apart from Daniel.

The problem was solved for her when two small boys raced past, pursued by their parents. She followed them to see what all the excitement was about. The excitement was about a dull-looking circle of red and white fabric on the floor. Stella was about to move away, until a toy demonstrator loosened a restraining strap, which caused the circle to pop up into a red and white space rocket, complete with engines and an observation window. The two brothers had a whale of a time testing the pop-up tent. It would make a perfect gift for Daniel, so Stella took one from the rack. She needed one more thing and asked the demonstrator for help.

Mission accomplished, the cashier parcelled her purchases up and Stella took them home, smug that she'd managed to find two gifts that Daniel would love. Now all she had to do was try not to count the days until her trip to Oxford to see the city of dreaming spires. It was a romantic name and she wondered whether the city would live up to it, or whether it would prove to be nothing more than a fancy backdrop for a purely platonic relationship.

Chapter Nine

At Oxford, Stella stepped off the train in the late-afternoon sun to find the Redmans waiting on the platform. Benedict took her rucksack and carrier bags while Daniel skipped at her side.

'Have you got me a birthday present?' he asked.

'Daniel,' intoned his father, 'it's bad mannered to ask for presents.'

Eyes downcast, the boy mumbled an apology.

Stella smiled. 'You'll have to wait until your birthday, little man, but I have made you some special birthday biscuits.'

'Ooh, have you? Can we eat one now, please?'

'When you get home. They're right down at the bottom of my bag, but as soon as I unpack, you can have them.'

Daniel beamed and swung on her arm as they walked to the car park, where she watched Benedict trying to open a mustard-coloured classic sports car by actually putting the key in the lock.

'Triumph Stag.' He shrugged. 'It's my one vice. To be honest, I hardly ever drive, except to the station now and then, and she does do a fairly reasonable number of miles to the gallon, especially considering her advanced years.'

'Relax,' said Stella, 'I'm not the environment police.'

'You might not be, but Miranda most definitely is the environment police. She loves to make me feel guilty so I'm always on the defensive when it comes to cars. I saw one of these in a James Bond film as a boy and wanted one ever since.'

Stella slid into a leather seat and ran her hand over the wooden dashboard that was punctuated with over half a dozen silver dials. This car from another age was beautifully made. Daniel hopped into the back and his father fastened the safety harness.

'Old Bessie's a bit of a boneshaker, I'm afraid, so if you've any loose fillings, the country roads should soon see them off.'

Fillings were something she didn't have, but to be on the safe side, Stella gripped the seat to either side of her. They drove through the city with a running commentary from Daniel about the weekend ahead, which guests were coming to the party, how he was looking forwards to jelly and ice cream and how he hoped for a sunny day so they could hold the party in the garden.

The city of Oxford certainly didn't disappoint and the sluggish traffic provided ample opportunity to take in the ancient and elegant buildings, with their many towers, spires and cupolas. They made their way through some of the university colleges, with Daniel excitedly pointing out where his father worked. In the sunlight, the yellow stone colleges glowed as if made of fairy-tale gold.

Before long, they were out of the city proper and driving through leafy streets, where large red-brick houses sat back from the road, their manicured lawns lolling before them. Benedict turned down a broad, tree-lined avenue and pulled into a drive. He climbed out of the car to close the gates behind them, unfastened Daniel and picked up Stella's bag. Together, they scrunched up the gravel drive towards a detached house with bay windows set either side of a bottle-green front door.

'Of course, it's too big for just the two of us, but I can't bear to part with it. We bought it when it was tumbledown, and Anna restored it…'

He didn't have to say any more. Clearly, Professor and Mrs Redman had hoped to fill this lovely house, with Daniel to be only the first of many children. It must be bittersweet living in the house with its memories of Anna tinged always with sadness. When she crossed the threshold, Stella was conscious that she was entering a home made by another woman. Far from feeling strange or upsetting, she felt as if Anna's spirit was welcoming her.

'Hello there.' Stella whispered, starting slightly as Benedict turned on hearing her voice. She shook her head as if to say she'd not said anything.

'Come on upstairs, and I'll show you to your room.'

Stella made to follow upstairs when a small figure squeezed past her.

'Daddy, please let me show Stella to her room. I helped to get it ready,' he added for her benefit.

The little boy led her to an airy room, which overlooked a back garden that was stocked with plenty of playthings. The room contained a dark wood bedstead, covered by an old-fashioned eiderdown. On the middle of the bed sat a battered yellow bear wearing a hand-knitted blue jumper.

She picked up the bear. 'And who would this noble chap be?'

Daniel blushed and held out his hands for the teddy.

'He's Tedward. He was Daddy's bear when he was a little boy, and now he's mine. My mummy knitted him this jumper to keep him warm because he has a baldy tummy.' In case proof were needed, Daniel raised the bear's jumper to reveal a threadbare torso. 'I put him in your room so you wouldn't be frightened in a strange room by yourself but now Tedward looks a bit sad in here.'

'That's because he must be missing you. Tell you what, how about you take Tedward back to your room, and I'll try to get along by myself? If it gets too much, I'll come and borrow him.'

'All right, then. But you won't need him, will you?' asked Daniel with a worried frown, clutching the bear to his chest.

Stella shook her head, trying to maintain a serious expression. 'I'm going to be fine. Look, why don't you sit on the bed and help me unpack?'

Stella opened her rucksack and started laying her clothes out in neat piles. She carried the piles to the chest of drawers, deliberately leaving a tartan tin on the bed. Daniel was taking a close interest in it, but having been told off once already for asking, the boy was clearly holding his tongue. Seeing Daniel's solemn face was more than she could bear, so she passed him the tin.

A wide grin spread slowly across his face. 'Are these my biscuits?'

'Indeed they are. Fetch them downstairs and we'll ask your daddy if you can have one with a glass of milk.'

He slid off the bed, his arms full of Tedward and the biscuit tin.

'Let me carry that tin until you make it downstairs.'

In the kitchen, Benedict had brewed a pot of tea and poured out a glass of milk. The three of them sat at the table while Stella opened the tin and offered the biscuits around. Daniel took one and studied it carefully, then dipped it into his milk before taking the biggest bite he could manage. Benedict took one and opened his mouth to take a bite, then paused to examine it more closely.

'You actually made him chocolate, cherry and broccoli biscuits?'

'It took a little while to figure out the recipe. The first time I put cooked broccoli into the mix, but it looked, smelled and tasted vile. So then I baked the biscuits and just before they cooled and set, I sprinkled them with buds of raw broccoli, and they're not too bad, believe it or not.'

'Eat up, Daddy. They're delish!'

'Delish, eh? Well in that case, I'd better eat this one before they're all gone.'

Benedict made a big show of being afraid to take a bite and clutched his throat as if poisoned. However, seeing Stella and Daniel's unimpressed faces, he finished eating without any further drama.

'Not bad,' he said. 'Not bad at all. One way of getting my five-a-day.'

Stella smiled. 'You'd have to eat an awful lot of biscuits, which would kind of defeat the object.'

'A good point.' Benedict leaned forwards and put the lid on the tin before putting it in a cupboard.

'We'll keep some for another day. Now, it's about time for someone's bath, teeth and bed. What do you say, Daniel?'

'All right, but will you read me a bedtime story, Stella? Me and Tedward?'

'If it's all right with your dad.' She looked to him for assent and he nodded. 'Just let me know when you're ready.'

The sound of happy squeals and splashing put her in mind of her own childhood bath times, of being lifted out of the bath and wrapped in a towel that had been warmed on the radiator. Enveloped in this way, she used to feel happy and secure, as if nothing bad could possibly happen in a world where she was wrapped in a warm towel.

From above, she could hear Daniel protesting about getting out of the bath, but Benedict clearly won the battle as she soon heard footsteps moving along the landing. She'd washed up and was wiping down the table when Benedict appeared, his shirt drenched.

'I thought Daniel was the one having the bath.'

'Yes, although you could be forgiven for thinking otherwise. It's always like landing a whale lifting him out. Well, he's shiny-faced, fluffy-haired and in his pyjamas if the story-reading offer still stands.'

'Absolutely. Any favourites?'

'He's very keen on *Horrid Henry* at the moment, and he

learns some of his best pranks from him, so read it at your peril.'

'Oh, I'm more than a match for Dastardly Daniel and Horrid Henry,' she replied as she made her way upstairs.

Stella had to read twelve pages of *Horrid Henry* before being allowed to leave the bedroom. She tucked Daniel in, with Tedward by his side, and kissed him on the forehead. She was struck by how angelic he looked. Ruffled hair, round pink cheeks, plump red lips, and those dimples – she'd been right about the Libran ascendant. She sighed, feeling for his mother who'd never known her lovely little boy. She was still gazing at his sleeping form when Benedict came into the room and stood next to her. They remained there for a short time, watching him and listening to his even breathing.

After a few minutes, Benedict drew Stella out by her elbow and pulled the door half-closed before treading softly down the stairs. Stella followed into the kitchen, where he began rattling about in the cupboards and the fridge. She took a stool at the central island and twirled round on it to watch, slightly bemused, as he lined up flour, sugar, butter, eggs and lemons on the counter.

'Are you baking a birthday cake by any chance?'

'I'm going to give it the old college try. Daniel wants a spaceship cake and I promised to get him one. Of course, there was no such thing in any of the shops so I planned to bake the cake tonight and do the decoration tomorrow night.'

'Do you need a hand?'

'No thanks. Miranda has already offered – it seems that nobody has any faith in my baking abilities. Got myself a recipe here and some designs from the internet. I mean, how hard can it be?'

'Not hard at all,' she said. 'But the offer of help stands if it all gets too much.'

Benedict propped up his tablet, then weighed and measured his ingredients, moving back and forth from the recipe to the scales. After a considerable amount of checking, adding and taking away from the bowl, he looked satisfied, although a little floury. Next, he picked up the ceramic bowl, ready to cream the butter and sugar together. He dug the wooden spoon into the block of butter, which, fresh from the fridge, scooted out of the bowl and shot across the floor. Without a word, Stella picked it up and dropped it into the stainless-steel pedal bin.

'You might try cutting the butter into small cubes next time. Assuming you've got some more.'

'Good thinking. Don't know why that didn't occur to me. There's more in the fridge.'

This time, he cubed the butter before adding it to the dish and started creaming again, more gently this time. After several minutes, all he had to show for his efforts were many mutilated cubes of butter, somewhat coated with sugar.

'Is this part meant to be so difficult?' he demanded.

'Not usually, but if you insist on using brick-hard butter straight out of the fridge, then you're bound to struggle. Here, let me help.'

Stella washed and dried her hands then plunged them into the mixture, rubbing the sugar into the butter with her fingers. Once the fat started to soften and her fingers started to get stuck, she pulled her hands out of the dish and pushed it back to Benedict with her elbow. While she washed her hands again, he started to cream the butter and sugar, with rather more success this time, and he looked quite delighted when the mixture turned to a grainy-looking cream. Encouraged by this small triumph, he picked up an egg and made to crack it on the side of the bowl and only Stella's sharp intake of breath stopped him.

'What now?'

'Sorry, nothing. Don't mind me. You just go right ahead.'

'If I'm doing something wrong, then tell me.'

'Well, if you just toss the eggs in, the mixture will curdle.'

He frowned at the eggs. 'And that's bad, is it?'

'Yes. Look, mix them up in a cup first, then just add a few drops at a time, and mix them in thoroughly before you add the next lot.'

He trickled in some egg and whisked.

'Like this?'

'Yes, just like that.'

Eventually, all the eggs were blended in.

'Lemon zest next?'

'If you like.'

Benedict washed his lemons and grated the zest into the mixture. He put his hand on the bowl of flour and looked up for guidance.

'You'll need to sieve it first to get rid of the weevils.'

'Weevils? But I bought this flour from the supermarket only a few days ago.'

'I know,' she laughed. 'I'm kidding. You just need to get rid of any lumps and make sure it's airy. So get sieving and then fold the flour in very gently so you don't knock the air out of the mix.'

He followed these instructions and poured the batter into two cake tins before putting them into the oven. No sign of any greaseproof paper.

'I'm impressed,' she said.

'Let's see how it turns out before we start the congratulations, shall we?'

'Fair enough, but short of a major burning incident, you should be fine. You do know not to open the oven door, I take it?'

'Stella. I'm hurt that you underestimate my culinary expertise by even asking that question.'

He was smiling broadly and had a rather fetching smudge of cake mixture on one cheek. She couldn't help herself and reached out to smear it off with her little finger before popping it into her mouth.

'Mmm, I take it all back, there's nothing wrong with this mix.'

He wasn't laughing now, but was staring at her and Stella felt frozen, finger in mouth as he took hold of her shoulders with floury hands and pulled her towards him. Every hair on her body stood on end as a shiver ran through her. He pulled her close and leaned in, and Stella's breath caught in her throat.

Suddenly, the door crashed open and a small boy with tousled hair appeared, clutching his teddy. 'Daddy, me and Tedward's scared. I had a nasty dream and now there's a big monster in my wardrobe.'

Benedict moved away from Stella with a trace of regret in his eyes as he scooped up Daniel and Tedward.

'Come on, let's go and check out that cupboard. Stella, do you want to come and help us do the monster hunting?'

'I'd love to, as long as it's not too scary.'

'It's definitely not scary is it, Daniel? We have a special monster zapper, don't we?'

Daniel managed a tiny nod. Benedict pointed at the vacuum cleaner in the corner and mouthed, 'Would you mind?'

Puzzled, Stella picked up the vacuum and carried it upstairs. Once inside the monster-infested bedroom, she put the cleaner down on the floor and awaited further instructions.

'Shall we let Stella get the monsters out of the wardrobe?'

Daniel, still clinging to his father, nodded.

'Stella, if you're not too scared, point the nozzle into the cupboard and turn on the monster zapper. You'll need to plug it in first, though.'

She adopted a slightly fearful but brave face, plugged in the hoover, turned it on and aimed the hose into the wardrobe, sucking for all she was worth, wrestling, grunting and fighting with the monster inside until she heard boyish laughter.

'Well that was certainly a very big and very mean monster,' she said. 'He was so hungry that he must have eaten all your clothes.'

'Goody, I hope he ate my uniform so I don't have to go back to school and can stay at home all the time!'

'Well, son, you've no school for a few more weeks yet, so no need to worry. Come on, Dan Dan, it's time to get back to sleep. What do you say?'

Daniel looked up, ready to appeal, but on seeing his father's stern face, gave in gracefully. Snuggling up to Tedward, he blew a kiss to Stella, who blew one back. Amazingly, after all the drama, he was soon asleep again and they returned downstairs. Stella was the first to notice the burning smell, and she ran to the kitchen. As she opened the oven door, black smoke billowed out. She jumped back before she got a faceful and put on oven mitts to extract the two cremated lumps. Benedict raced to the back door and opened it, wafting the smoke out with a tea towel.

'If Daniel gets a whiff of this, we'll have another nocturnal visit. How bad is it?'

'Pure carbon, I'm afraid, and only fit for the bin.'

'Typical luck and that was the last of the eggs. How am I going to bake another cake and decorate it in time now?'

'I'll buy more eggs in the morning and bake another cake before Daniel gets up, ready for you to decorate in the evening.'

'Stella, I can't ask you to do that – the shop's over a mile away.'

'I'll be going for an early morning run anyway and may as well make myself useful.' She suppressed a yawn. 'Speaking of an early start, it's way past my bedtime.'

'You go on then. I'll tidy the kitchen and lock up. See you in the morning.'

Stella wondered if she should kiss him goodnight, but the moment had passed, and he seemed hopelessly distracted by the burned cakes.

'Goodnight, Benedict. See you in the morning.'

'Sleep well, Stella.'

Once she was ready for bed, she slipped beneath the warm quilt and snuggled into the soft pillow. The room was warm, but there was a cool breeze coming through the sash window, which was slightly open at the bottom and top. It was perhaps the first time in her life she'd seen a sash window that was actually operational and not painted shut or held open with a block of wood. Outside, the night was quiet and the only sounds came from inside the house as Benedict softly moved about turning off lights and locking doors.

As she drifted away to sleep, she couldn't help thinking about the near-miss kiss earlier. That hadn't felt platonic. What would have happened if Daniel hadn't woken up? Maybe, just maybe, they were destined to be more than friends.

Chapter Ten

Stella removed the butter from the fridge and left it to reach room temperature then set out in the pink glow of dawn to find an open shop. She had to do an extra lap until the shop opened at seven, but managed to get her eggs, along with one or two other baking necessities. Back at the red-brick house, she let herself in with the spare key Benedict had left out for her with a little note. Typically, it gave nothing away, saying only *Spare Key* followed by a smiley face. Once indoors, she stowed her provisions then padded upstairs to take a shower. Today was going to be a laid-back sort of a day so she dressed in jeans and her favourite red jumper. It had many holes in it, which she'd darned over with daisies. The end was in sight for it because soon there would be more daisies than jumper, but it was still just about wearable.

Downstairs in the kitchen, she checked the oven temperature, hunted out the utensils she'd need and measured out her ingredients by eye. Everything from the wooden spoon through to the cake tins had been chosen with care, and she tried not to think too hard about the woman who'd equipped her kitchen ready to bake birthday cakes for her future children. There was even a colourful set of spoons and whisks designed for small hands. She creamed the sugar together with the room-temperature butter, and within quarter of an hour she was pouring fragrant batter into a pair of duck-egg blue baking tins and sliding them into the oven.

By the time she'd finished washing up and tidying away – a task that always took much longer than the actual mixing part – a lemony smell started to fill the kitchen. She guessed the cakes were ready and gently opened the oven door for a peek. Seeing they were indeed ready, she pulled the door wide, donned the oven gloves and lifted the beautifully risen golden sponges onto some cooling racks. The sight and smell of the cakes made her hungry, so she'd have to get on and make some breakfast. By the sound of the thumps and clumps coming from upstairs, someone else was also ready for breakfast. Just as well she'd bought plenty of eggs.

While the eggs boiled, she ground some coffee beans and set the pot on the hob to brew, then squeezed three oranges and put the jug and tumblers on the table. After testing the sponges with the back of her hand to make sure they were cool enough, she stashed them in a high cupboard so Daniel wouldn't see them. Benedict came into the room, sporting a piece of what looked like newspaper stuck to a shaving injury on his chin.

'I'm a dreadful host, expecting you to bake and then letting you make our breakfast too.'

'It's fine, and it makes a pleasant change to have someone else to cook for.'

'Well, it's still very good of you.' Benedict patted his cut chin. 'I'd better go and hurry Daniel along. He was deciding which socks to wear when I left him, and it can take all day sometimes.'

Typical for a child with a Libran ascendant thought Stella to herself. Always delightful but seldom able to choose between two things.

When Daniel ran into the kitchen, clutching Tedward,

there was a neat stack of toast soldiers on his plate, along with a perfectly soft-boiled egg. Daniel was wearing two different socks, and Stella gave him a quizzical look as she poured out some orange juice.

'I can't decide if spotty socks or stripy socks are my favourite, so I'm wearing one of both.'

'I see. Wearing one of each sounds like an excellent solution if you can't make up your mind. Come on, get stuck in.'

She chopped the top off his egg, and the little boy dipped in a buttery soldier. Within seconds, he had egg yolk smeared around his mouth. Benedict came into the kitchen, now minus his wound dressing, and grimaced at the sight of his son's face.

'Daddy, we're having dippy egg and soldiers.'

'Yes, I can see that. Except it's more like drippy egg, judging by the state of your chops.'

Stella nudged Benedict towards the table and passed him a plate before joining him. The sun shone through the window and lit up father and son's hair with golden lights as they razored their way through breakfast.

'A bit hungry, are we, Professor and Master Redman?'

'We certainly are, aren't we, Daniel?' Receiving a yolk-smeared smile and a nod in reply, Benedict continued. 'It's been so long since anyone cooked us breakfast. I can't remember when…'

'Aunty Miranda makes dippy eggs and soldiers all the time. She made them the other week.'

'For you, Daniel. I was away. You stay at Aunty Miranda's sometimes, don't you?'

'Mm-hmm. Aunty Miranda's nice, I've got my own bedroom in her house, Stella.'

'Have you? I bet it's a lovely one too.'

'Yes, it is, because it's all painted a lovely green colour, like an apple, and she's got a big tree in her garden that she lets me climb when Daddy's not looking.'

'Does she? Well Aunty Miranda sounds like a lot of fun. Is she coming to your party?'

The boy nodded. 'Daddy, will Aunty Miranda bring me a present?'

'Almost certainly, but I beg you not to ask her about it. I can't face another lecture on the importance of good manners in children.'

Daniel scraped his spoon against his plate, and when his father got up to fetch more coffee, he whispered loudly in Stella's ear.

'Stella, I bet you've brought me a great big present.'

'Daniel Redman! What did I just say about asking for presents?'

'But I wasn't asking, Daddy. I was just guessing.'

'Daniel…'

At his father's tone, the boy moved away from Stella, his little cheeks glowing. She gave him a sympathetic wink. Poor kid was just excited. Still a little sheepish from his father's ticking off, Daniel excused himself from the table and asked if he could play in the garden. When granted permission, he grabbed Tedward and ran outside to play.

It was a perfect summer morning and the powder-blue sky was scattered with fluffy white clouds. Tangles of flowering shrubs framed and sheltered the lawn. At one end was Daniel's climbing frame, complete with a swing, slide and monkey bars. Stella could see Daniel from the kitchen window as she washed up beside his father. Watching him playing on the swing, with Tedward on the grass looking up at him, she thought what a lonely little boy he must be, with a father who had to work away a lot and an aunt acting as a stand-in mother. What he needed was a chubby puppy. This was definitely a boy in need of a dog to love and mess about with. She handed the newly clean pan to Benedict to dry and emptied out the washing-up bowl.

'Did you ever think of getting Daniel a dog?'

'What?' Benedict turned suddenly. 'You haven't bought one for his birthday have you?'

'Of course not.' This sharp tone was a bit disconcerting. 'Is he allergic or something?'

'No, but Miranda is absolutely terrified of dogs. She can't bear them.'

'But she doesn't live here.'

'No, but she has Daniel whenever I'm away, and she could hardly be expected to take in some mangy mutt as well.'

What kind of person didn't like dogs? Miranda Redman, evidently – no surprises there, then. Stella wiped down the table and hung the dishcloth over the tap to dry then excused herself to the garden to play with Daniel. Mangy mutt, indeed!

From the garden, where she was busy pushing Daniel on his swing, Stella watched his father through the kitchen window. He was frowning at a piece of paper, then weighing out ingredients with the precision of a pharmacist. He must be planning to ice the cake while the birthday boy was otherwise occupied so she was careful to keep Daniel facing away from the kitchen window.

Almost an hour later, Benedict came outside and Stella raised an eyebrow at him, pointing at some disturbing grey sludge on his cheek, which he scrubbed off with one hand.

'So,' she said, almost afraid to ask. 'How did it go?'

'Not bad. Not bad at all. I've done a reasonable job – it's just like fixing the walls when they develop the odd hairline crack. I've hidden my handiwork in a high cupboard.'

When Daniel raced over to ask his father what handiwork was, Stella grabbed him and threw him to the lawn before lying on the grass next to him and pointing up at the sky.

'Come on, Daniel, let's look for space monsters.'

'Ooh, yes! Daddy, come and help us look for space monsters.'

'Space monsters?'

'Yes, Daddy, honestly. Space monsters.' Daniel pointed to an overhead cloud. 'Look!'

'Um, yes. Right, good one, Daniel!'

'Daddy, you're pretending again, I can tell. You have to lie down to see them. Tell him, Stella.'

'Your son is right, Benedict, you have to lie down to see the space monsters properly. Come on down, the lawn is lovely.'

Benedict folded himself down onto the grass and stared up at the sky.

'Look, Daddy, look. There's a good one. Can you see it? It's got horns on.'

'Oh, yes,' he said. 'I see it now. You know you're right, you do have to lie down to see them properly.'

Stella turned to grin at Benedict over Daniel's head.

'Does that mean I'm forgiven for being the only dog-hating Englishman in the country?'

'I don't know about that,' she said. 'We'll have to see.'

Benedict still didn't look too sure about the space monsters in the clouds, but it was pleasant lying on the warm grass, with the perfume of roses and honeysuckle wafting over them, surrounded by the gentle hum of insects and the chirruping of birds. The air rustled through the leaves on the overhanging trees and Stella was struck by how delightful the simplest things could be when there was time to stop and enjoy them. Something she didn't do nearly often enough.

Benedict pointed to the sky. 'Look,' he said, nudging his son. 'There's a three-headed, googly-eyed space monster up there, with furry feet! Quick, or you'll miss it.'

Stella and Daniel giggled at this clumsy attempt at joining in.

'I most certainly do not have three heads and googly eyes,' said a woman's voice, 'and my feet could never be described as furry.'

Stella sat upright and found herself faced with a bemused Miranda pushing a bike through the gate, its basket and panniers laden with shopping bags. Hessian shopping bags, by the looks of them. Daniel jumped up and raced towards his aunt.

'Aunty Miranda. Aunty Miranda! Are those my birthday presents?'

'Certainly not, young man, and you might do well to remember that boys who ask seldom receive.'

'Sorry, Aunty Miranda.'

'You're forgiven as it's your birthday and you're excited. Now, will someone kindly explain what the three of you are doing down there?'

Benedict was already on his feet, brushing grass from his clothes. 'Just doing a spot of space-monster spotting. You've sort of met Stella before, in Greenwich. Stella, this is my twin sister, Miranda.'

'Pleased to meet you, Stella,' said Miranda, not sounding the least bit pleased. 'Would you like to give me a hand with this lot?'

Stella got up to lend a hand with the bags. She was not looking forwards to this. In the kitchen, she placed the hessian bags on the kitchen counter. It was a relief to put them down as they were remarkably itch-inducing, to say nothing of their strange odour.

'I've fetched some food for tomorrow,' said Miranda. 'My brother, if left to his own devices, will feed the guests from packets, boxes and plastic bags.'

Stella watched as Miranda unpacked her provisions and filled the fridge with what looked like half a farmer's market worth of fruit and veg. She was no expert in children or their preferred party food but was willing to bet her tax rebate that spinach didn't feature very highly on most kids' top ten. There again, Daniel had a penchant for broccoli, so maybe his aunt did know best.

'Miranda, can I ask you something, please?'

'Can I stop you?'

Stella hated putting herself on the back foot with this woman, but given the sensitivities around this weekend, she didn't want to burden Benedict.

'Will your parents be coming? Only, your brother doesn't mention them much.' In fact, he'd never mentioned them once.

'They won't be coming, and I strongly recommend that you don't ask Benedict to open that particular can of worms, especially not this weekend, or at any time, come to that. And you mustn't mention them to Daniel. As far as he's concerned, they're on a round-the-world trip and have been these last seven or so years.'

'I won't say anything. Not to anyone.' What was that all about though? How odd that Daniel had never met his paternal grandparents.

With the subject of her parents closed for discussion, Miranda stood on a step to reach a high cupboard, peered in and pulled out a large, molten-looking grey lump. Turning it this way and that, she frowned.

'Don't tell me my brother has been trying to bake?'

Miranda walked briskly towards the gleaming bin and placed the toe of one shoe on the pedal to lift the lid, poised to throw the grey lump in.

'Wait!' Stella yelped and ran to rescue what she now realised was the cake she'd baked that morning and which Benedict had attempted to decorate. In response to a perfectly groomed and arched eyebrow, Stella pointed out that it was Daniel's birthday cake. 'It's meant to be a spaceship.' Although the casual observer could be forgiven for failing to notice that, she supposed.

'There was never any need for Benedict to waste his time. He knew fine well I'd ordered a cake from the organic co-op. None of its ingredients have travelled more than five miles.' She paused for a moment. 'Well, at least they hadn't until just now, but I was coming this way, and it was by bike.'

She retrieved her offering from a hessian sack. The cake had very little to recommend it, apart from the fact that it looked exceedingly high in fibre.

'It'll be lovely once it's decorated,' said Stella, lying

through her teeth. 'I bought some marzipan this morning, and you're welcome to–'

'Marzipan? With actual almonds?' Miranda inhaled for such a long time, it appeared she might damage a vital organ. 'You do know that it takes a whole gallon of water to produce a single almond? Eight pints of water for one nut. And don't get me started on almond milk.'

'Never touch the stuff,' said Stella, determined to rescue the situation. 'It'd be a shame to throw away this cake after Benedict worked so hard on it – grey and tragic though it may be. It won't take me long to tidy it up.'

'Stella, the only thing that would tidy up this abomination would be a very hungry and unfussy dog, and there's no chance of any dog – hungry or otherwise – setting foot in this house as long as I'm here.'

'Well, waste not, want not.' Before Miranda could slide the cake into the bin, Stella prised the tin from her hands and returned it to the cupboard. No wonder Benedict had seemed so distraught by the burnt offerings the night before.

'Suit yourself.' Miranda turned to fill the kettle. 'I'm making tea, would you like a cup?'

Stella would have preferred coffee but felt she wasn't being given the option, and also wasn't prepared to be lectured about the distance the coffee beans had travelled. Probably less far than the tea, come to think of it, unless this woman was planning to brew her own nettle tea or something. But she kept that thought to herself in the interests of maintaining the peace since she was only a guest here.

'Yes please. Tea would be great.' It wasn't even afternoon yet – what would Benedict think?

'So, you're the amazing Stella that we keep hearing so much about? I must say that both Daniel and Benedict appear quite taken with you. Of course, it can't go anywhere as I hear you're off to pastures new in a few months. Just as well you haven't got yourselves too involved. It would be painful for Daniel to be let down, don't you think? So it's good that you and my brother are just friends, isn't it?'

Despite the barrage of questions, Stella felt yet again that she wasn't being offered the right to reply. The law had been decreed and she was expected to fall in line.

'Although,' Miranda said as she placed crockery on a tray, 'I was rather surprised to hear that you'd been invited to Daniel's birthday tomorrow, because you know what other day it is, don't you?'

'Yes,' said Stella. 'I do, and it will be very hard for Daniel and Benedict.'

'Not only for my brother and nephew. Anna was my closest friend ever since uni. We met at Cambridge, and I introduced her to my brother.'

Stella groaned inwardly. 'I didn't know that.'

'No reason why you should, but it's not me that I'm worried about. Anna's parents are very close to Daniel and they always come to his birthday parties. It's a terrible anniversary for them too, because they lost their only child that day. So you understand my surprise at Benedict thinking it would be acceptable for you to be here. You know, on a day like tomorrow when all of us present will be grieving for Anna, except you.'

'I had no idea. I'm so sorry.'

'No need to be, this is just characteristic lack of consideration by my brother. You seem like a nice girl, Stella, and I know you wouldn't want to be responsible for hurting two elderly people, would you?'

Stella shook her head. 'I shouldn't have come.'

'Agreed. You shouldn't have come. Listen, if you want my advice, the best plan for everyone would be if you discreetly made your excuses and went home after lunch.'

While Miranda was a truly horrible woman, she was also probably right.

'But won't Daniel be upset that I've left?' Stella was torn between wanting to do the right thing and not disappointing the little boy.

'He'll be a whole lot more disappointed when you leave him and move on to your next flat-sitting assignment. Canada, I believe? Best to get it over with now. Don't you agree?'

'I hadn't really thought about that.' Stella had thought about it but didn't want to give this harridan the satisfaction. She couldn't believe she was allowing herself to be spoken to in this way, but now Miranda had occupied the moral high ground, there was nothing to do but surrender.

'No, I don't suppose you had thought about that, Stella, and I don't suppose my brother had either. It's just as well that Daniel has one sensible adult looking out for him. When you get home, please consider what possible harm you might be doing by staying in his life. Do the right thing and make a clean break.'

With that, Miranda swept out of the kitchen with the tray, leaving behind one cup on the table. A clear message that Stella wasn't welcome in the garden, so she took her tea over to the window and watched Daniel swinging upside down from his monkey bars. With a sigh, she poured the tea down the sink, washed and dried her cup, put it away and went upstairs.

Weighed down by a strong sense of regret, Stella knew she had to do the right thing. Miranda was right and staying around would only cause more pain when she moved on. Moving on was what she did. It had been stupid of her to think of getting involved with anyone, let alone someone with a child, and especially one so vulnerable. As painful as it might be for everyone, it was better to go now. It would have been lovely to see Daniel enjoying his birthday, but Miranda was right about one thing: her presence would be a dreadful burden on his maternal grandparents. Even accounting for Benedict's absent-mindedness, it was odd that he hadn't mentioned his in-laws would be coming.

She lifted her rucksack down and started to fold her clothes, planning to leave a note making her excuses, along with Daniel's presents. It was terrible sneaking away like a

coward, but there was no real choice. She was leaning on
her rucksack, trying to fasten the straps, when there was a
tap at the door. Guiltily, she turned around and stood in
front of her bag. Benedict came in, took one look at her
packed bag and anger flared in his eyes.

'I'm sorry,' said Stella in a small voice.

'You have nothing to be sorry about, and you needn't
think you're going anywhere either. Unpack that bag at
once.'

'But I have to go back immediately, you see—'

'Please don't insult my intelligence with a lie. You don't
have the face for lying – you're as red as your jumper. Are
you going to tell me what my dear sister has been saying to
you?'

'Um. Well, um.' Stella didn't want to tell tales, but she
didn't want to lie either.

'Then you leave me no option.'

He turned on his heel and marched from the room.
Stella's heart sank as he left. She'd really blown things and
now Benedict was so angry that he'd walked out on her. She
had been planning to call a cab to take her to the station but
after this little scene, she didn't want to hang around any
longer than necessary, so she'd walk to the main road and
catch a bus instead. The sooner she was gone, the better it
would be for everyone.

In the garden below, Daniel continued swinging by
himself, but there was no sign of his father or his aunt. A
door opened and closed downstairs and there were angry
words spoken in hushed tones – clearly for Daniel's sake. It
was impossible to hear what was being said, but it went on
for some time and ended with the front door slamming,
followed by the sound of a bicycle being wheeled quickly
down the drive. There was a creak on the stairs. Stella held
her breath, wondering if she was next to be evicted.
Benedict walked into the room, without knocking this
time.

'Apologies for my sister's behaviour. I've sent her

packing, and if she gives a repeat performance at the party tomorrow, then the same thing will happen.'

'Your sister has a point though. I don't want to upset Daniel's grandparents, or hurt Daniel when I move on, not when he's lost so much already. Miranda's right and it's better that I go now.'

'Oh, Stella. Anna's parents will never get over the loss of their daughter. I'll never get over the loss of my wife. Daniel will never get over the loss of his mother. But life has to go on, and Daniel would be upset if you weren't at his party tomorrow – you're his guest of honour, you know. As for when you move on, how about we cross that bridge when we come to it?'

Stella's head was still telling her to walk away for everyone's sake, but her heart had ideas of its own, so she nodded.

He stepped back. 'I'd better go down to check on Daniel. Why don't you unpack and join us? I'm making some coffee, and we can finish off your broccoli biscuits with it.'

'All right,' she said. 'I won't be long.'

Feeling a little brighter, she hung up her clothes again, wondering how she'd manage to deal with this dreadful twin sister. Being protective was one thing, but Miranda behaved like an over-zealous bodyguard. Since the bodyguard had been exiled for the time being, Stella would worry about her tomorrow and not before. In the meantime, she'd try to enjoy the remainder of Saturday and let Sunday take care of itself.

Benedict fetched a tray of coffee and biscuits into the garden with a glass of milk for Daniel. As they sat in the sun munching and drinking, Stella noticed the tea tray that Miranda had taken out earlier, abandoned near the shed. Either it was too early in the day for tea, or it had been nettle tea after all.

'What do you want to do with your day,' she asked Daniel, 'on your last day of being six?'

'Well, when I was in that place with the castle – what was it called?'

'Durham.'

'Yes, Durham. It was brill when we went on the river in the boat, but we never got to see any frogs. Can we go to our river and see some frogs, Daddy?'

'Indeed we can, but we'll need to decide where to eat. What would you like to do? Have some lunch here or go out somewhere?'

Daniel frowned. 'I don't want to do either of those things. Can we have a picnic instead?'

'We can, little man, but only if you help to make it. Stella, stay exactly where you are. Despite being guest of honour, you've never stopped since you got here. Relax, enjoy your coffee and don't move so much as a muscle while the Redman men prepare a feast.'

Chapter Eleven

Picnic agreed on and wicker hamper packed in the boot, they drove for an hour through winding, narrow lanes lined with tall hedgerows. It was amazing there weren't more traffic accidents in the countryside, given the tight bends and the way people whizzed around them. Stella glanced at Benedict's profile. While he dealt with Daniel's never-ending questions, his eyes never once left the road, careful to protect the precious life in the back of the car.

They started playing I spy, and Daniel's I-spy-something-beginning-with-f was causing a few problems. After exhausting flowers, ferns, fox (unfortunately dead on the side of the road), friend (Stella, apparently), factory, farm, fingers and forehead, the adults were forced to admit defeat.

'Fumb!' announced a triumphant Daniel.

'Fumb?' asked Stella.

'Fumb,' said Daniel, holding one up by way of example so his father could see it in the rear-view mirror.

'Son, you mean thumb.'

'Yes, that's what I said, fumb.'

Stella turned round and grinned at him. 'What a funny little boy you are.'

'Daniel, you haven't said fumb since you were four. Besides, a thumb is a finger, so technically Stella won that round. Now, how about seeing who can spot the most yellow cars?'

They passed the last fifteen minutes of the journey with Daniel scanning the road and periodically shouting, 'yellow car'. Before long, they pulled into a small car park. Benedict jumped out and held the door open for Stella then unfastened Daniel. He took the hamper from the boot and pointed down a small track through some trees and dense undergrowth.

'Here we are: the Isis. When I was a boy, we used to swim in the river along here. There's a sort of natural pool near a sunny glade, surrounded by some excellent climbing trees. Shall we try there for frogs, Daniel?'

'Yes please, Daddy.'

The path was narrow, and Benedict had the hamper to contend with, so Daniel held Stella's hand. The boy jumped and hopped as they made their way along the shady path, with his father holding low branches out of their way where the path was badly overgrown. When they arrived at the promised glade, Benedict unpacked the hamper and arranged the food on the picnic blanket. As they munched on boiled eggs and ham sandwiches, insects buzzed around them and fish jumped in the river, making occasional plops. Daniel was drawn to the water, but his father told him he wasn't allowed near the edge on his own and must wait until everyone had finished eating. Once they'd shared out the home-made biscuits and finished with a crunchy apple apiece, Stella cleared away and packed up while Benedict took his son behind a bush. Before long, Daniel emerged from the bush, carrying a particularly large caterpillar to show Stella. After she'd admired it, his father explained that if he carefully put it back where he'd found it, within a few days it would turn into a chrysalis and then metamorphose into a butterfly. Daniel failed to look impressed.

'Oh, Daddy. I know all about chrysalises and

metamorphothingy. We did it in nature study at school. Honestly!'

After harrumphing at his father's lack of knowledge about his schooling, Daniel carried the caterpillar back to its original leaf. Stella suppressed a laugh at the serious expression on the boy's face, but gave in at the sight of his two little feet sticking out from under the bush as he grunted and groaned, shuffling back to exactly the spot where he'd found the caterpillar. When he reversed out, his knees were muddy, his T-shirt was torn, and he had twigs and leaves in his hair.

'Now I know why they say people look like they've been dragged through a hedge backwards,' said Stella. 'Come here, untidy one, and let me clean you up.'

Determined not to be cleaned up, the grubby scoundrel ran to his father, who picked him up in a bear hug, gave him a big kiss and swung him round until Daniel was almost crying with laughter. Then he held him close and told him that he loved him.

'I love you as well, Daddy.' Daniel pressed a kiss onto his father's cheek.

'Now, let's see if we can find some frogs. Come on, Stella.'

The three of them ventured to the riverbank where they lay down and peered into the mud. After a while, Benedict reached down and when he raised his hands, they were cradling a frog. He showed his son how to cup his hands so that he wouldn't drop the small creature. The boy's eyes shone as the frog hopped in his hands until Benedict retrieved it and returned it to the mud.

'Goodbye, Hoppy. It was nice to meet you,' said Daniel, waving as the frog hopped off. 'Daddy, I didn't know you could catch frogs.'

'I can do lots of things that you don't know about, son.'

'Do them, Daddy. Do them, please!'

'Just for you, then.' Benedict ran to the nearest large tree, his son in hot pursuit. With astonishing ease, he climbed the branches as if they were rungs on a ladder, and within a few seconds was sitting on a high branch, swinging his long legs. Daniel, at the bottom of the tree, was doing his best to follow, but he couldn't make it up to the first branch. Stella lifted him onto the lowest bough and he sat ten feet beneath his father swinging his little legs in the same fashion.

'Come on, Stella,' called down Benedict, 'there's a branch up here with your name on it.'

Despite not having climbed a tree in over twenty years, Stella needed no second bidding and soon found herself sitting on a branch, lower than Benedict, but higher than Daniel. It was shady among the leaves and she enjoyed the cool air for a while, engaging in a face-pulling contest with Daniel, until, with a sickening crack, the branch gave way beneath her and she fell backwards through the air. Her stomach lurching, she scrabbled at passing branches, but they rushed through her fingers. Briefly, she registered first Benedict's horrified face and then Daniel's looking down on her. Next, there was a hard thump and everything went dark. She opened her eyes to find Benedict's face swimming in front of her and she could hear Daniel crying in the background.

'Stella? Stella? Are you all right? Can you speak? Have you hurt your head?'

She felt sick, there was a terrible pain in her arm and she could only croak.

'Head's fine. Wrist not so much.'

'Do you think it's broken? Oh, Stella, I'm so sorry. I'll make a sling until we get you to the car. There's a first-aid kit there so I can patch you up properly then get you to hospital. Or do you need an ambulance? How are your legs? Can you feel them?'

'Legs feel all right.' Her wrist throbbed but it didn't feel broken. Hopefully, it was just a sprain.

Benedict gently brought her up to a sitting position, and kneeling behind her, took off his shirt and folded it into a makeshift sling. As he reached from behind to tuck his shirt under her injured arm, Stella, through her pain, was aware of his bare chest against her back, warm even through her jumper. And there was that lovely nutmeg fragrance again. She inhaled deeply.

'Sorry, did I jar you?'

'No, no. It's fine.'

Benedict finished tying up the shirt and moved in front of her to check the sling before helping her up. Although she winced at the pain caused by moving, she enjoyed the feeling of his hands supporting her, and also the glimpse of his bare chest. He stooped to pick up the picnic hamper.

'Daniel, please walk behind me and in front of Stella so we can make sure you don't fall in the river. We've had quite enough accidents for one day.'

Slowly, they made their way back to the car in single file, with Stella bringing up the rear. While her wrist did hurt, she was more dismayed at ruining what had promised to be a lovely afternoon. Plus, she'd have to go back to London and miss the birthday celebration as she'd be neither use nor ornament with her arm out of action when there was a party to oversee. She took her mind off her woes by admiring Benedict's shoulders, which were broad for someone so fine-boned, and she had to resist the urge to reach out and touch his bare skin with her good hand.

Back at the car, Benedict helped Stella into her seat, retrieved the first-aid kit and started to make a replacement sling. He crouched before her and managed to fit the proper sling without her feeling the slightest twinge, and she watched with considerable regret as he put his crumpled shirt back on.

'I'm going to take you to the nearest hospital with an A&E, but first I'm going to call Miranda and ask her to meet us there to collect you, Daniel.'

In response to his son's immediate protest, Benedict pointed out that they could be in A&E for hours and it would be a dull way for a boy to spend a Saturday afternoon. He called Miranda, and it was obvious that things were far from easy between them. When they left the car park, Benedict drove with a furrowed brow, quickly but carefully and without jerking Stella's arm, despite the country roads.

After what felt like an age, they pulled into the hospital car park to find Miranda waiting for them. Benedict climbed out of the car and exchanged a few words with his twin, then helped Daniel out of the car and leaned down to kiss him.

'Aunt Miranda's going to take you home and stay there with you until we get back. If we're not there by bedtime, promise me that you'll be a good boy and go to bed nicely for her.'

Daniel promised and waved sadly from the rear of his aunt's car. Stella waved back with her good arm, feeling bad for ruining the little boy's day out with his dad.

Stella had been tested for concussion, prodded, poked and X-rayed before being fitted with a steel-backed wrist splint that was covered in garish pink foam. As suspected, it was only a sprain, so she'd got off pretty lightly, all things considered. It was after six when they returned and Benedict helped her from the car. Miranda had eaten with Daniel, then bathed him and now they were halfway through his favourite *Horrid Henry*. Stella was sore, tired and not looking forwards to another confrontation with the snappy sister. Perhaps sensing this, Benedict asked if she wanted to rest, suggesting that he could get dinner ready while she napped. Grateful for his consideration, she headed upstairs to nurse her injured pride, but Miranda started before she was even out of earshot.

'I can't believe how irresponsible you are, climbing trees at your age. What if Daniel had been hurt too? She'll need to go home first thing in the morning. You'll be busy, so I'll drive her to the station and put her on the train. Save you the bother.'

Stella couldn't hear Benedict's reply but she felt too weary to compete with this woman who was so evidently determined to get rid of her. Grateful to be out of the way for a while, she lay on the bed, trying not to listen to the voices downstairs, but she could hear Miranda's sharp tones whether she wanted to or not, which meant that the little boy could also hear.

A couple of minutes later, she heard a car driving off. With Miranda gone, she felt better already. Maybe she would close her eyes for a short time. Her mother had always claimed that sleep was the best medicine.

When Stella woke up and went downstairs, she paused in the doorway. In an armchair, Benedict sat with Daniel on his knee, holding the boy's book in front of him, running his finger underneath the words as he read. He put on lots of funny voices to make Daniel laugh and would occasionally stop before a word that he knew his son could read and wait for him to say it. Together, father and son said, 'The End'.

'Right, come on, Daniel. Finish your milk and we'll get you off to bed.'

'Can't I say goodnight to Stella? I thought she would have come in to see me.'

'She's very sore, son. She needed to have a little rest, but she'll be a lot better in the morning.'

'She's a lot better now, actually.' Stella walked into the room and sat down in the other armchair. 'That nap did me the world of good.'

Daniel scrambled down from his father's knee, put his chubby little arms around her neck and pressed milky lips to her cheek.

'There, I've kissed you better. Daddy always kisses me better, don't you?'

'I most certainly do.'

'Daddy, why don't you kiss Stella better? It might help her arm to mend quicker.'

'Er, well, I think kissing things better only works on children, you know. Come on, son. Off to bed with you.'

'No, Daddy. That's not true, because when you're poorly I kiss you better and it works. So if you kiss Stella it will work. Won't it, Stella?'

Stella had to look down at the floor to hide her grin.

'Ooh, I don't know, Daniel. Maybe your daddy's right. Perhaps it does only work on children, or when children give you a kiss. Anyway, your kiss is already working its magic on my arm, so I'm fine for the time being.'

'All right then,' said the boy, not looking entirely convinced. 'But if your arm's not better in the morning, Daddy will have to kiss you better.'

'That's a deal. Now, best let your dad take you to bed. You've got a busy day tomorrow.'

'All right. Goodnight, Stella.'

'Goodnight, Daniel.'

Benedict hoisted his son and carried him upstairs. Stella could hear the distant sounds of teeth being brushed and Daniel still discussing the merits of kissing things better. For one terrible moment back then, she'd thought he was going to insist on his mortified father kissing her better, and she could just see the earnest child overseeing the entire operation. Even though it hurt her bruised ribs, she couldn't help laughing.

Benedict came back into the room, looking appalled. 'I must apologise for my son's mouth running away with him. In his defence, he is only six.'

'Only for one more day though. That was the funniest thing I've seen in ages. Your face was a vision of pure horror. I never thought the idea of kissing me would frighten anyone so much!'

'Oh, I wasn't at all scared at the idea of kissing you. It's just, well, you know…'

'I know, Benedict, I know. But he was so straight-faced and innocent. I may have cracked a rib laughing.'

'Don't say that, or you'll make me feel even more guilty.

I've been the worst possible host, haven't I? You've had to bake cakes, cook breakfast, contend with my sister, and as if that wasn't enough, I managed to half-kill you during a picnic. No one would blame you for leaving and going home. Not that I want you to go home,' he added quickly. 'Far from it.'

'In that case, I'll hang around. Anyway, speaking of cooking and baking, what are we having for dinner?'

His face fell. 'Oh, I'd not even thought about that. Would you mind a takeaway?'

'Always happy to eat a takeaway.'

He opened the middle drawer in a nearby dresser and fished out a handful of menus.

'You know there's an app for that, right?'

'Oh, this collection took years to build so I'm rather attached to my menus. Anything in particular you fancy?'

'Surprise me,' she said, cursing herself for putting her foot in it. He and his wife had probably used those very menus and he couldn't bear to throw them away. 'I'll eat pretty much anything so long as it's not nuclear hot.'

'Duly noted.'

'While we wait, I'll finish decorating Daniel's birthday cake if you like.'

'No need. I iced it this morning and it's ready.'

'Yes, I saw how ready it was when Miranda was about to scrape it into the bin.'

'What?' He turned towards the kitchen. 'She'd better not have.'

'No, she didn't. The cake is safely back in the cupboard. As for being ready, I don't mean to be cruel, but letting Miranda put the cake out of its misery might have been the kindest thing. It is a bit pathetic looking, you've got to admit.'

'Come with me and we'll see.' Together, they went into the kitchen where he lifted his masterpiece out of the cupboard and examined it, grey icing and all. 'Seeing it in the hard light of early evening, you might have a point.' He set it down on the counter. 'Poor Daniel. He desperately wanted a spaceship cake and I've let him down.'

'It only needs a few tweaks to fettle it. I could have a go if you like.'

'With only one good arm?'

'I think we can safely assume that my one good arm is better than your two when it comes to matters culinary. In fact, I reckon my one *bad* arm is probably better than your two good ones. Go and order some food and let me rescue this sorry-looking specimen.'

Benedict left to place a phone call and then returned to the kitchen.

'I've ordered a good mixture, so there's bound to be something we both like. Turns out we've hit the takeaway rush hour, so it's going to be at least ninety minutes, but I doubt you're in danger of fading away any time soon...' Seeing her eyes widen at this remark, he barrelled on. 'Still, on the plus side, it gives us more time to fix the cake, though I do think you'll struggle with only one hand.'

'Smooth,' she said. 'Nearly as smooth as your icing job. Now, if only you had a cake-stand, the icing would be a doddle. I don't suppose...'

'Not a cake stand, as such, but I might have just the thing. Back in two ticks.'

Overhead, Stella heard him tiptoe into his son's room and wondered what he could be looking for. He soon returned, still on tiptoe, like a triumphant burglar.

'Here you are. One potter's wheel, courtesy of Daniel's toy box. Might need a bit of a wash though. My son tends to take the act of clay throwing quite literally.'

Once the potter's wheel was cleaned, he set it on the counter in front of Stella and lifted the cake onto the turntable. Although designed for throwing clay, the wheel was also perfect for icing cakes.

'Not bad, clever clogs,' she said. 'Not bad at all.'

'I've been called worse. So, shall we ice?'

'We shall.' She grinned at him. 'Or rather, I shall while

you make yourself useful knocking up some new icing, if you can do that without wreaking too much havoc. But maybe try to be a bit more imaginative with the colour scheme and let's not just have fifty shades of grey this time.'

Oblivious to the reference, he turned to the cupboard, muttering. 'I think you'll find it's silver since all spaceships are silver, according to Daniel.'

Poor kid. Daniel might have been better off with the high-fibre low-excitement cake that his aunt had bought rather than this misshapen monstrosity. While Benedict mixed a rainbow of colours, Stella scraped off the lumpiest parts of the existing icing and smoothed down the sides of the cake. Because Benedict had been so ham-fisted, he'd somehow managed to gouge a large hole in the top layer of the cake and he'd simply filled it in with about half a pound of butter icing. She could get away with slicing the top layer off and having a shallow cake, but it would look as if the cake hadn't risen, and she was taking no chances with Miranda about. She was still busy examining the cake this way and that when Benedict presented her with a tray containing an icing bag, a pint pot filled with more grey icing and several teacups filled with coloured icing in various hues.

'I'll start by covering the cake again.' Stella pointed at the pint pot. 'Let's start with that grey stuff.'

'Spaceship silver, I think you mean.'

'Hmm.' She raised her eyebrows. 'Can you hold the pot while I scoop it out, please?'

She quickly spooned the grey icing onto the cake and smoothed it off with a palette knife.

'Amazing! In a matter of seconds, you've covered the cake perfectly. Although, you do seem to have made a terrible hole in the middle. Still, you are working with just the one arm.'

She turned to give him an old-fashioned look. 'Don't push your luck, Redman. While that's drying, I need you to make some shapes. Watch me.'

She cut a block of marzipan into eight and kneaded a different coloured dye into each, then rolled a piece out and cut five little shapes from it with a paring knife. They spent a silent half hour rolling and cutting, with Benedict struggling to keep up with Stella, until they were left with a jumble of multi-coloured shapes that didn't resemble anything in particular.

'Right, Benedict, you'll need to help me with this part. I'm going to decorate the cake and you need to rotate the turntable. But first, can you fill the icing bag with some more of that gr– er, spaceship silver.'

Once in possession of the filled icing bag, Stella positioned herself on a high stool, close to the counter, with her partner in crime standing behind her, reaching forwards to move the turntable slowly round while she iced as best she could. She could feel him very close behind her, breathing on her neck. It took considerable will-power not to lean back against him. Instead, she tried to concentrate on the job but was struggling to squeeze the icing out with just one hand. She leaned into the bag to get at a particularly tricky bit. This overbalanced her and she fell back on Benedict, who caught her easily with a firm grip on her waist. There was a long pause while neither of them said anything. Slowly, he swivelled Stella around to face him. Because she was on a high stool and he was standing, their eyes were almost at the same level. This was it. He was definitely going to kiss her. Just as he leaned towards her, the doorbell rang. He smiled into her eyes and kissed her on the nose.

'Saved by the bell. Don't move. I'll be right back.'

What abysmal timing. It hadn't even been an hour, let alone an hour-and-a-half. Was that a thing now for restaurants – to under-promise and over-deliver? While Benedict tipped the delivery driver, she wondered what would have happened if they hadn't ordered food? Might Benedict right now be carrying her upstairs to his lair, draped over his arms like a swooning heroine? He certainly had the shoulders for it, but did he have the knees? Knees were all important when it came to stairs. Especially when the swooning heroine was apparently in no danger of fading away anytime soon. When he returned, his arms were laden with small boxes.

'That's a lot of food, Benedict. Are you expecting guests?'

'No, it's a banquet for two. I wasn't sure what you liked, so there's some of everything. Fork or chopsticks?'

'Chopsticks, if you've got them.'

'Chopsticks it is. Definitely some around here somewhere.'

While he located the chopsticks and organised the food, Stella quickly assembled the remaining parts of the cake and made the finishing touches. The final result was from her usual standard, but there was a limit to what could be achieved with a sprained wrist and an incredibly kissable man within her good arm's reach. She couldn't manage to lift the cake into the cupboard with only one hand, so she pushed it into a corner and turned a tin upside down over it, arranging some boxes on top so that if Daniel came down early in the morning, he wouldn't know what it was.

She joined Benedict at the table, which was dotted with small cartons. Now that there was nothing more exciting on the menu, she was looking forwards to eating. Benedict seemed all business again, and it was as if the near-miss kiss had never happened. The food smelt delicious and she dug in, briefly contemplating whether she could get away with feeding him a pot sticker from her chopsticks, but the combination of unfamiliar eating implements and using her less dominant hand for eating made her think better of it. She was halfway through a piece of prawn toast when Daniel appeared at the bottom of the stairs. Stella indicated to Benedict with her eyes that they had company.

'Yes, Daniel,' he said, without turning his head. 'What can we do for you?'

'Is it my birthday yet, Daddy? I can't sleep. And I can

smell delish smells and they're making me hungry so can I have some please?'

'Very well, seeing as it's your last couple of hours of being six, you can stay up just this once. Do you want a fork or chopsticks?'

'Ooh, chopsticks, chopsticks!'

Benedict fished out another pair and tucked Daniel into his chair at the table. Stella smiled as he chased his food with a chopstick, eagerly trying to stab it.

'No, son. Like this. Watch.' Benedict held his large, lean hand over Daniel's small chubby one and showed him how to pick up his food. Despite his efforts, Daniel couldn't quite master it so Stella downed tools in solidarity. Stretching out her good hand, she picked up a dumpling.

Daniel took a sharp breath. 'Stella, fingers!'

'I'm sorry for my table manners, but it's late, I have a bad arm, it's past your bedtime and it's nearly your birthday. So just this once, I reckon we can use our fingers. What do you say, little man?'

Daniel looked to his father for permission, which Benedict gave with a resigned smile. Now that there was definitely no chance of romance, Stella decided to dig in. Benedict shrugged and threw his chopsticks down on the table, pretending to fight over the last piece of sesame toast, but allowing his son to win. Finally, after they'd worked their way through rice, cashew chicken and soft noodles, they sat back, full and happy.

'It's getting very late, Dan Dan. How about some milk and then upstairs for teeth and bed?'

'Oh, not teeth again. I did them already.'

'Yes, but that was before you ate your own bodyweight in noodles.'

'If I do the drinks,' said Stella, 'will you two do bin duty?'

That should keep the kid out of the kitchen and away from his cake. Within ten minutes, they were all back at the table nursing either a glass of milk or a cup of jasmine tea.

Stella inhaled the fragrant steam and felt its soporific effects working on her almost immediately. She smiled sleepily and stifled a yawn. Benedict smiled back and tapped Daniel on the shoulder.

'Come on, son. Up the wooden hills with you.'

'Can I sleep in your bed tonight? Please, Daddy?'

'Only for tonight, because you're a big boy now. We'll let Stella go to bed and you can help me to lock up. Say goodnight.'

'Goodnight, Stella.'

Daniel closed his eyes and puckered his lips, so Stella leaned over and kissed him lightly on the cheek. She wondered whether she could lean over a little further and kiss his father just as casually. Maybe not.

'Goodnight, birthday boy. Goodnight, birthday boy's dad.'

From her bedroom, she could hear father and son brushing their teeth together. She lay back and thought about the near-miss kiss earlier. Things had been so normal afterwards, it was as if it nothing had happened. Well, nothing had happened, she reminded herself, which was hardly surprising with the anniversary of Anna's death on the horizon.

Chapter Twelve

Stella awoke to the smell of sausages sizzling, surprised at oversleeping as she'd had a nap the day before and was usually such an early riser. When she got up to go to the bathroom, she heard Benedict whistling in the kitchen. As she reached the head of the stairs, he must have heard her.

'Back to bed, Ms McElhone. I didn't set my alarm an hour early on a Sunday to make you breakfast in bed, only for you to come downstairs and eat it. Go. Consider that an order, please.'

'Going, going, gone.'

She nipped into the bathroom – she might be having breakfast in bed, but she wasn't going to be dishevelled. One-handed, she rinsed her face, brushed her teeth and smoothed her hair as best she could without a comb, then dashed back to bed just as Benedict appeared, teacloth over one arm, bearing a tray. On it was a coffee pot, orange juice, a plateful of sausages, tomatoes and mushrooms, and a smaller plate of toast, butter and honey.

'This looks lovely, thank you.' It also looked like a lot to put away after last night's takeaway. 'What about Daniel?'

'His is in the warmer. He'll sleep for a few hours yet after such a late night, which is just as well since he's got a long day ahead of him. Let me know when you've demolished that little lot and I'll run a bath for you.'

'No need, thanks. A shower will be fine.'

'Not with that splint. If it gets wet, it'll go nasty, and you're not to take it off for at least a week. Am I right?'

'You are, but I'm capable of running my own bath, thank you.'

'Don't worry – I wasn't planning on bathing you. Go on, get stuck in, because there'll be nothing until party food after this.'

The sun streamed through the window, a light breeze billowed the curtains, and she had a tray in front of her prepared by a man who'd set his alarm early so he could surprise her with breakfast in bed. There were worse ways to start the day.

As good as his word, Benedict drew Stella a bath and she was delighted to see that he'd sprinkled red rose petals from the garden into the steaming water. Getting into the bath while not putting any weight on her bad arm or getting it wet proved something of a challenge, but she managed it, balanced her sore wrist on the side of the bath, and lay back to let the steam and the roses go to work on her bruises and aching muscles. There was a tablet of amber soap that looked as if it had been hewn from a large block. Likely something from Miranda's organic co-op. If it was, it was a lot more tempting than the cake, and Stella relished the spiced fragrance as she lathered herself. Nutmeg. So this soap was the source of Benedict's heavenly smell. Once clean, she lazed in the water and planned her party outfit. She'd packed a lavender linen shift that was pretty enough to wear for a party without being too formal. Fortunately, it was sleeveless, so getting it on wouldn't be too difficult.

Once she was out of the bath (with some difficulty, and accompanied by the fear of slipping and having to be rescued – naked – by Benedict), she dried herself and got dressed. This was easier said than done, especially when it came to zipping up her dress. Once fully clothed, she despaired at the allegedly flesh-coloured splint, which would be fine for anyone whose flesh was actually the colour of pink ointment, but its lurid hue ruined her outfit. Inspired, she took out her new cream silk camisole set and tucked one edge of the camisole into the end of her splint, wound it round a couple of times and tucked it in. Still far from ideal, but at least it looked a bit less ugly, and there was absolutely zero chance of her needing luxury lingerie for any other purpose this weekend.

She combed her hair and dried it before adding a touch of violet scent to her throat. Her mother had worn this simple flower essence, and although she didn't have her any more, she could breathe in her memory. She took a steadying breath, reached into the wardrobe and took out the presents so Daniel could have them when he got up as he'd be over-excited at the party, and too many presents in one go might overwhelm him. Stella clamped the pop-up tent under her bad arm, and with the other present in her good hand, she made her way downstairs to the kitchen.

'You look an absolute vision, Stella. That colour really sets off your eyes.' Benedict coughed and nodded at the gifts. 'And it looks like Christmas has come early. You really didn't have to, you know.'

'I know, but I wanted to.'

'Here, let me take them from you. Oh, I like what you've done with the splint. Very tasteful.'

Tasteful considering she was basically flashing her underwear. Still, no one needed to know that.

He set down the presents. 'I'd better finish off the birthday cake so you don't risk your nice frock with food dye.'

'No need. I finished it last night while you were sorting out the takeaway. It's not perfect, but once we get the candles and sparklers on, no one will notice.'

'Where is it? Can I take a look?'

'If you're quick, because I think someone's on the move.'

Stella raised her eyes to the ceiling at the sound of creaking floorboards.

'Ah, maybe not in that case. I'll go and make sure he's all right. Back in a sec.'

Father and son came downstairs a short time later. Daniel was still in his pyjamas, hair ruffled into little spikes, looking even sweeter than usual. He was seven today but still had babyish features.

'Hello, Stella.'

'Good morning, Daniel. Happy Birthday! Are you ready for breakfast?'

'Mm-mm.'

He wriggled his way up onto a high stool at the island, and Benedict put a plate of breakfast in front of him.

'I bet you're not the least bit hungry after your midnight feast.'

'No, I am hungry. I can easily eat all of this. Watch me.'

The little boy started to wolf down his breakfast at an amazing rate.

'Easy, tiger,' said Stella. 'You might want to slow that down or you'll be hiccupping all day.'

Daniel grinned and kept eating. 'I want to eat fast so I can get on with my birthday faster. Daddy says I've got to go and get dressed in my party clothes, but I want to stay in my pyjamas today because it's my birthday.'

'Won't your guests find it a little strange if you're still in your jim-jams? They might think it's bedtime and go straight home,' pointed out Benedict.

'Hmm, I never thought of that. All right then, I'll put my birthday suit on.'

Stella and Benedict grinned at each other.

'What?' Daniel looked from one to the other. 'What's funny?'

'You are, son. You are. Come on, let's go and get your birthday suit on.'

'Can't I have my present off Stella first?'

'Daniel, I thought we'd agreed: no more asking for presents.'

'Sorry, but I can't wait another minute.'

'Well, as it happens, Stella was about to give you your present after breakfast, but only once you've finished your sausages.'

'Mmmmm.' Daniel started chomping his way down a sausage like a small buzz saw, keen to get to the present. Once finished, he placed his knife and fork neatly together in the centre of his plate and looked up expectantly, a streak of ketchup on his chin.

Stella produced two parcels, both wrapped in navy-blue paper scattered with golden stars, and handed over the first package. Daniel dug in his fingers and started trying to rip and shred the gift-wrap, but it wasn't budging, so Benedict knelt at his side to help. It was such an odd shape, and it had taken yards of sticky-tape to secure the wrapping. With a final tug, Daniel pulled off a long strip of paper. When he saw what was there, he gasped and looked at his father in wonderment.

'Daddy, it's a goldfish bowl. Am I getting a goldfish?'

Benedict examined the gift. 'Why don't you keep unwrapping and find out?'

With wide, shining eyes, Daniel tore off the remaining paper. 'It's not a goldfish bowl. It's a space hat!'

'Yes, it's a space helmet,' gently corrected Benedict.

'And a spaceman suit as well. Can I wear it instead of my birthday suit? Can this be my birthday suit?'

Before anyone could answer, Daniel was shrugging his arms and legs into the costume. Benedict fastened the back and helped him into the helmet. The visor moved up and down, but stopped short above his nose. The suit had integral boots and Daniel started space-walking around the kitchen, hunting for aliens.

Benedict leaned forwards and whispered. 'Thank you, Stella. It's not often he fails to notice he has another present waiting for him. It's perfect, but you really shouldn't have spent so much.'

'It wasn't so much, and besides, I couldn't resist. Hey, Daniel, don't you want to open your other present – although, we should probably open this one in the garden.'

Daniel turned round in slow, gravity-free motion and space-walked to the kitchen door.

Outside in the garden, Stella laid the second present on the lawn and Daniel knelt down and set about removing the paper. This one had been easier to wrap, so it was much easier to open. Daniel pulled the paper off in one go and threw it aside. He looked slightly disappointed at the puddle of red and white nylon lying on the grass.

'Thank you, Stella, but what is it?'

'Let's find out. You need to stand well back though. Next to your dad. We're going to count down, all right?'

Kneeling down, Stella waited for Daniel to huddle next to his father, then once he was in position, she began.

'Ten, nine...' she was joined loudly at this point by Daniel and they continued together, '...three, two, one. Blast off!'

At blast off, she released the fastening and the tent popped up.

'It's a rocket! Thank you, thank you! This is my best present ever!'

He dashed inside his rocket and a few seconds later the little astronaut peeped out of the observation panel.

'I can go to the moon in this, you know,' he shouted. 'I'm ready to blast off again. Myryooooggghhh. I'm off to the moon.'

'Very good, son, but make sure you're back in time for lunch. Thank you, Stella, for such lovely presents – they're going to be a hard act to follow, and I'll struggle to persuade him he can't wear his spacesuit to bed.'

'It's great to see him looking so happy. He's an adorable little boy, and you must be so proud of him.'

'I am. Very proud.' Benedict touched Stella lightly on her hurt arm. 'How's your wrist?'

'A bit sore, but much better than yesterday. Thanks for taking me to hospital and staying with me, I know it can't have been easy for you to be there, especially not at this time of year... sorry.'

Stella was afraid she'd veered into difficult territory and looked down at her feet. Benedict caught her chin and raised her face to look at him.

'You don't have to be sorry about anything, Stella, and I wouldn't have been anywhere else yesterday. Besides, getting you patched up was the very least I could do in the circumstances.'

He looked into her eyes, and despite the warm morning sun, Stella felt a shiver run through her. Was he going to kiss her now? Instead, he laughed, his eyes crinkling against the sun, and tapped her nose with a finger.

'Anyway, can't stand about all day when I've got party favours to pack. Think you can help if I bring everything out here? I doubt we'll get Daniel back inside before dark.'

'I'll do my best. How many kids are coming?'

'Only half a dozen or so boys, a couple of girls and a few adults, so it should be fairly civilised.'

Stella crossed her eyes at the thought. Seven, seven-year-old boys? Civilised? Hadn't this man ever read *Lord of the Flies*?

One hour later, the party bags were packed, and Miranda had arrived and set to work in the kitchen preparing the party food, refusing all offers of help. She peered at Daniel haring round the garden in his spacesuit and playing in his rocket.

'I see someone's been rather spoiled today and isn't going to appreciate his other presents. To say nothing of all the man-made materials involved. You know, they have those rocket tents in cardboard.'

Stella didn't retort, even though the admonishment was directed at her, but Benedict came to her rescue.

'Between your nephew and the English weather, cardboard wouldn't last two minutes, Miranda, and he is over the moon with his presents.'

'Well, let's see this cake then,' said Miranda, refusing to concede. 'I shudder to think what the pair of you have concocted. One of you scarcely knows his left hand from his right and the other has a strapped-up wrist – hardly a recipe for success, is it? Fortunately, there's always my shop-bought one.'

'Yes,' countered Benedict, 'I've seen your shop-bought cake. It looks so dense it could give your average black hole a run for its money. Look, I appreciate your help, sis, but why don't you take some of Stella's home-made lemonade and relax in the garden for a bit?'

It was pleasantly said, but Benedict's jaw had tightened. Miranda walked straight past the lemonade and pointedly helped herself to a glass of water instead. As she passed, Stella felt a strong urge to stick out a foot and trip up the evil twin, but it seemed unwise, given the fact that she was a barrister. Benedict followed his sister into the garden, clearly intent on having few words, and Daniel came indoors shortly after, red-faced and panting.

'Stella, I'm thirsty, can I have a drink please?'

'Of course you can. Milk or lemonade?'

'Ooh, is it that lemonade you cooked before?'

'It is. Want some?'

'Yes, please.'

'One freshly cooked lemonade coming right up.'

She handed Daniel a glass and he immediately stuck his hand in, pulled out an ice cube and started sucking it happily.

'What a cheek. I've just been conned. You didn't want a drink at all. You just wanted the ice. Come on, birthday boy,

I've got something else to give you before your guests arrive.'

'Brill, is it another present?'

'Kind of. Let me nip upstairs to fetch it. I won't be long.'

On her return, Stella handed Daniel a scroll bound with a green bow. He pulled the ribbon off and unrolled it, pointing excitedly at the illustrations adorning the horoscope that Stella had drawn for him.

'It's a bit like a map of the sky when you were born.' She pointed to a little circle with a dot at its centre. 'See, this is the sun, and when you were born, it was sitting near a group of stars that look like a lion. So anyone born around this time of year is a Leo the lion.'

Daniel didn't look particularly convinced but was happy to practice being a lion and prowled around the kitchen on all fours, trying out a few experimental roars. When he tired of being a lion and sat down to drink his lemonade, he ran his finger over the coloured lines linking all the planets. Stella explained how each planet in the sky played a part in life on earth, just as her mother had taught her.

'But how can they, Stella, when the planets are so far away?'

'Well,' she racked her brain, trying to think of the best way to put it. Her mother had been much better at this than she was. 'Think about the sun, Daniel. What does the sun do?'

'Emm…' He stuck his tongue out and looked up at the ceiling while he pondered. 'Emm, it keeps us warm?'

'Yes, it does keep us warm. And what else?'

'Umm. Does it make things grow, like the grass and bread and things?'

'Good. The sun warms us up, helps things to grow and keeps us alive. It looks after us and makes us happy. So, who does the sun sound like? Who looks after you and makes you happy?'

'Daddy does!'

'That's right, so the sun is a bit like a daddy.' She

decided to skip the moon's connection with motherhood. 'And the moon. The moon is pretty magical too. Do you know what the moon does?'

'Phoo. This is hard. It's like being at school.'

'Sorry, Daniel, I didn't mean to make you work so hard on your special day. We can stop if you like.'

'No, no. Tell me what the moon does. I give in but still want to know.'

'You know at the seaside, how the sea goes in and out, backwards and forwards?'

Daniel nodded solemnly. 'Yes, I've seen it loads of times on holiday.'

'Well, that's the moon doing that; it pulls the water backwards and forwards.'

'How does it do that?'

She smiled at him, half wishing she'd not started this.

'It's a bit like a big magnet, I suppose.'

'But the sea's not made of metal, Stella. Even I know that. We did magnets at school in science and you've got to be made of metal for a magnet to work.'

'Well… you've got a point there.'

'Stella, let's go and ask Daddy. He knows all about moons and stuff, and he'll tell you it's not like a magnet. Come on.'

With that, Daniel ran off and Stella rolled up the birth chart, taken aback at how quickly she'd plunged out of her depth. She hadn't recalled giving her mother such a hard time when they'd had similar conversations, but then Stella wasn't the child of a professor, and it was clearly going to be a case of like father like son. Daniel tore across the garden towards his father.

'Daddy, Daddy! Guess what, guess what! Stella thinks the moon's a big magnet. She says it makes the sea move about even though everyone knows the sea's not made of metal.'

Miranda was lying back in a deckchair, fanning herself with the Sunday newspaper, and she peered over the rim of her sunglasses. Stella, feeling like a naughty schoolgirl, tried not to shuffle her feet.

Benedict frowned. 'Steady on, Daniel. Slow down, take a deep breath and tell me again.'

Daniel stopped, took a theatrical deep breath, and then blurted out exactly the same sentence at the same speed.

'What makes you think Stella's not right, son?'

'Because the sea's not made of metal,' said Daniel. 'It's made of water and fish.'

'Right...' Benedict looked up at Stella, and raised an eyebrow. 'And what has the sea being made of water and fish got to do with anything?'

'Well, if the moon's a magnet and it pulls the sea around, then the sea has to be made of metal. We did magnets at school.'

Laughing, Benedict swooped up his son and flew him through the air.

'Come on, spaceman, let's send you to the moon and you can see what that's made of. Red cheese?'

'Noooooooh!'

'Blue cheese?'

'Noooooooh!'

'Green cheese?'

'Yeeeeeees!'

Benedict punctuated each question with a swoop through the air, making Daniel shriek with delight.

'Someone missed out purple cheese.' said a kindly voice. Immediately, Daniel wriggled out of his father's arms and dashed towards the garden gate.

'Grandpa, Grandpa! I thought you weren't coming.'

'We were always coming, Daniel, but we got stuck in the most awful traffic jam.'

'Grandma, Grandma!'

'Hello, darling. 'Sorry we're late. Have the terrible twins been behaving themselves?'

Daniel's grandmother bent to hug her grandson and kissed him seven times in rapid succession.

Daniel giggled and whispered, 'Yes, but Aunty Miranda keeps fighting with Stella.'

'Does she now, and who wins?' said his grandfather.

'Stella does most of the time, but she's got a poorly arm today so she's not as tough.'

'Then we might have to help her out, but for now let's see if we can find everyone, shall we?'

Grandpa Bob picked Daniel up by a leg and an arm and swung him to and fro as they walked down the path towards the back garden.

'Hello, everyone. Sorry we're so late. Shocking traffic for a Sunday.'

'Hello, Bob. Catherine.' Miranda wound herself past the swinging Daniel to kiss each of them in turn. 'Put him down, Bob. He's getting over-excited. He's already being cheeky, and we don't want any tantrums today.'

Grandpa Bob reluctantly put Daniel down. Benedict came over to shake his father-in-law's hand and to hug his mother-in-law.

'Hello, you two, you're getting younger-looking every time I see you – retirement must agree with you both.'

'I don't know, Benedict. Twice as much husband and half as much pay – retirement's not all it's cracked up to be.'

Catherine was smiling fondly at her husband, and it was clear that she was delighted to have twice as much husband around. Stella warmed to the friendly couple immediately.

'What's this we've been hearing about a certain someone being cheeky? Surely not our lovely grandson?'

Daniel blushed and Stella winked at him.

'It's nothing,' said Benedict. Just a misunderstanding about the moon and tides. Stella was right you know, son, about the moon controlling the sea.'

'Yes, Daniel, it does. And it controls all the water in you too,' added his grandmother, tickling Daniel under the arms and making him guffaw, in spite of Miranda's disapproving eye.

'Does it, Grandma?' Daniel gasped and looked in wonderment at his body. 'What about lemonade?'

'Yes, lemonade too,' she said. 'Do you want some?'

'Yes please, Grandma, with ice cubes as well. Lots of them.'

'You stay there, Catherine,' said Benedict. 'I'll fetch lemonade for everyone, complete with plenty of ice cubes for you, Daniel. But first, I'd like to introduce you to Stella.' He turned around and drew her towards his in-laws. 'Bob and Catherine, this is my friend, Stella McElhone. Stella, meet Bob and Catherine Telford, my in-laws.'

'Hello, my dear, very pleased to meet you.' Catherine leaned forwards to kiss Stella. 'I must say, you're very brave joining the circus today.'

'Pleased to meet you, Stella.' Bob shook her good hand with a firm grip. 'A certain dickie bird tells me you live within a stone's throw of my favourite cricket ground.'

'Ah, yes,' she said. 'Lord's is just up the road from me.'

'Honestly, Bob,' said Catherine. 'Can't you go thirty seconds without mentioning cricket? And just look at the poor girl's arm. You won't be throwing any stones with that for a while. What happened, my dear?'

'It's a long story, but basically my tree-climbing career is over.'

'I rather thought it might be something like that. Benedict, you need to take better care of your friends, or you might end up not having very many.'

Chastened, Benedict went off to fetch the lemonade. Catherine sat down in a garden chair and patted her knee.

'Daniel, come on over and give me a cuddle before your friends get here.'

The little boy jumped onto her knee and snuggled in. As his grandmother kissed his ears and whispered to him, stroking his hair and soothing him, Stella had to hold back a sigh for this family, somehow managing to live without their wife, mother and daughter. Although Anna was no longer here, she must be very much missed.

As Daniel was busy with his grandparents, Stella went to help with the lemonade. Benedict was dropping ice into glasses as she came in.

'Sorry about that, Stella. I should have forewarned you. When my son gets over-excited, he can become quite impertinent. He wouldn't normally speak to anyone like that.'

'Don't worry about it. Obviously, he has a scientific mind.'

'Yes, although I'm not sure what Miranda's excuse is. I'll have a word with her.'

'Please don't. It might make things worse, and I'm easily big enough and ugly enough to take care of myself.'

'Don't say that about yourself when you're anything but big. You barely come up to my shoulder.'

'Charming! How did you get to be so mean all of a sudden?'

She flicked an ice cube across the bench at him, he caught it and shot it straight back, Stella did a magnificent one-armed save and slammed it against the counter where it broke in two and shot off in different directions just as Miranda entered the kitchen.

'If there's any ice after you two children have finished playing, I wouldn't say no to another glass of water.'

Resigned, Stella left the twins to it and headed back out to the garden. On seeing her, Daniel jumped off his grandmother's knee.

'Stella, will you push me on the swing, please?'

'I will.'

Daniel climbed onto the swing and looked up at Stella with a serious expression.

'I didn't think you'd want to push me because I wasn't very nice teasing you about the sea not being made of metal. Aunty Miranda says it was bad-mannered and that you might not like me any more. You won't stop liking me will you?'

'I'll always like you, Daniel. And if you think someone's

wrong, then you're right to challenge them. Never be sorry for asking questions. You're not bad-mannered at all, just a lovely little boy who's getting a bit impatient waiting for his party to start.'

'I know, it feels like it's been ages. What time is it now?'

'After twelve, so your friends will be here soon. How about ten more pushes and then maybe Grandpa could read to you for a little while?'

Bob had a book-shaped present with him and the Telfords might like some quiet time with their grandson before the party. Daniel agreed and Stella started to push him, counting each push. Within seconds, he was giggling again and pushing his legs back and forth. On her final push, he shouted out 'ten' and launched himself off the swing in mid-air.

'Daniel, you'll hurt yourself.'

But he landed like a cat and sprang upright immediately.

'I always fly from the top – it scares Aunty Miranda.'

Well, at least Stella had one thing in common with his aunt. Daniel squeezed between his grandparents, and Bob held out an oblong present, which Daniel happily unwrapped.

'It's the new one! Thank you, Grandpa and Grandma. Will you both read it to me, please?'

As she watched Daniel nestled between his grandparents, their heads resting gently against his, Stella was struck by how small and vulnerable he was. It saddened her to think he'd fretted about being bad-mannered – Aunty Miranda was quite a piece of work.

Chapter Thirteen

The peace was soon broken by the sound of approaching children. Daniel leaped to his feet to check out the noise, his book and grandparents immediately forgotten. Two small boys with curly brown hair – one taller than the other – fought their way up the garden path, followed by a harassed-looking man carrying a brightly wrapped parcel. It was Nasty Nigel. Evidently, he'd found someone who didn't think he was that nasty if they were prepared to conceive not just one child with him, but two.

'James, stop pulling Nathan's hair. Nathan, stop pinching James. Hello there, Stella. Fancy seeing you again, and here of all places, on today of all days. James! Don't make me tell you again.'

Truly, a most unpleasant man, and the acorns had fallen not too far from the oak by the looks of things. At the bottom of the garden, Daniel and both of Nigel's sons were now attempting to ride the swing at the same time, and Stella briefly wondered whether it could take the strain. If it couldn't, she reasoned, they'd only fall a couple of feet onto the grass, and since they were sure to survive, she left them to get on with it. Before long, the garden started filling with an assortment of boys, two girls and a handful of parents.

The children amused themselves by chasing, fighting and laughing. Before five minutes had passed, one small boy was in tears and his mother was attempting to console him. Benedict circulated to ensure everyone had drinks and glanced Stella's way to make sure she was all right. She was fine and quite happy chatting to those parents who weren't Nigel, all of whom appeared to be friendly. But when she went into the kitchen to get some water, she found herself cornered by the unpleasant man, who decided to bend her ear on a few of his pet topics.

Given his captive audience, Nigel seemed to think it was a good use of his time to outline an astronomy grant application. While Stella was interested in the planets, she found it impossible to muster any interest in form-filling. Despite her lack of response, he insisted on telling her that he and Benedict were bidding for several million pounds so they could hold their own in some European research programme that Stella couldn't begin to understand.

Bearing in mind she was a guest in someone else's home, that a child's birthday party was underway and it was the most difficult of days for several of those in attendance, Stella did her best to be polite – a quality that seemed to evade Nigel. This man was difficult with a capital D. Besides being able to bore for England, he kept grilling her about her relationship with Benedict, which made her uncomfortable, not least because she wasn't sure there was any relationship to be grilled about. When Benedict finally came to her rescue, she smiled gratefully at him.

'Hello, you two. The children have run themselves ragged, so I'm going to sit them down for lunch in the vain hope that Miranda's organic banquet might have a calming effect.'

'Strongly doubt that, old man, but I admire your optimism. Stella here has been telling me all about your weekend.'

Benedict raised an eyebrow, but before Stella could put him right, Nigel was off again.

'Must say, rather bad form to invite someone over and then break their arm. Should have come to me, Stella, I know how to look after girls like you.'

Stella edged away from the leering man. 'Benedict's looked after me perfectly well. Besides, it's only a sprain. Anyway, Nigel, it was... interesting to meet you again.'

'Likewise, Stella. Catch you later.'

Not if she had any choice in the matter. Stella moved off with Benedict, relieved to be out of Nigel's way, but not wanting to speak out of turn, since the two astronomers were colleagues. As they approached the children – all nine of whom were currently attempting to cram themselves into the rocket tent – Benedict waved his arms to attract everyone's attention.

'Kids, come on. Time to eat.'

The children cheerfully ignored him, gave up on the tent and started fighting their way around the garden. Miranda stood up and clapped her hands together, which quickly got everyone's attention.

'Children. Lunch. Now.' Immediately, they stopped playing, fell silent and moved as one towards the picnic table.

'That's more like it. Now, who's for a glass of green slime?'

Stella knew she should probably admire Miranda's firm and confident manner, but she couldn't help feeling the joy had been sucked out of the garden as all the little people sat quietly at the table saying please and thank you as they passed party fodder to and fro. As they ate and the parents alternated between pouring out green slime and mopping up green slime – which at least explained the crop of spinach in the fridge – Benedict stood next to Stella and patted her on the shoulder.

'Thanks for putting up with us all today. It's hardly been a roses and champagne sort of weekend, has it?'

'I'm not really a roses and champagne sort of girl, and at least the kids have diluted the ice-queen's evil presence.'

'Stella, you are wicked. Although she does bring it on herself – when Miranda ordered the children to sit down, quite a few of the adults almost sat down as well.'

'Does the military know about your sister? She could go far.'

'Mmm, it's tempting, but she might cause a diplomatic incident.'

She laughed. 'Speaking of diplomatic incidents, the jelly and ice cream's all gone.'

'Then it's time the birthday cake made its grand entrance. Come and help me arrange the candles.'

Checking no one was in imminent danger of being tied up or drenched with green slime, they headed for the kitchen, where Stella unveiled the remodelled cake.

'It's fantastic. How did you manage that?'

'I was inspired by the terrible hole you made.' She arranged seven candles around the crater and placed sparklers in the middle. 'All done. Now, off you go.'

As Benedict carried the cake out, Stella noticed Miranda's superior glances as she cleared a space in front of her nephew and prepared to sneer. Benedict set down the cake and stood back.

'I forgot the lighter,' he mouthed and dashed back to the kitchen.

'Wow, Stella, did you make my birthday cake for me? It's brill. Look, everyone! My birthday cake's in the shape of the moon and it's got aliens and spaceships on it and the big crater's got a space-lion in it.'

'Doubt it's a lion, kiddo,' remarked Nigel, leaning over for a better look. 'After all, there are no lions in space.'

'But there is a lion in space,' protested the boy. 'Stella told me that when I was born, the sun was next to Leo the Lion in the sky, so I'm like a little lion but with really big teeth.' As if to prove it, Daniel threw back his head, bared his teeth and roared at Nigel.

'Leo the lion?' Nigel rolled his eyes. 'Stella must be a bit of an astrologer, eh?'

'Yes, she is. Just like you and Daddy.'

'No, son. She's not at all like me and Daddy. Look, here he comes now with the lighter. Benedict, old boy, you didn't tell me you were hanging about with fortune-tellers these days – I say, Stella the Fortune Teller!' He sniggered at his own joke. 'And you seemed such a sensible-looking girl, too.'

Stella was about to take the bait, but remembered she was at a children's party and smiled through gritted teeth instead. She wasn't sure whether Benedict had heard the jibe, but judging by Miranda's delighted expression, she'd certainly heard it. Fortunately, Daniel was too busy examining his cake to notice the barbed comments flying overhead. While Benedict lit the candles and sparklers, everyone gathered around to sing 'Happy Birthday'. When they'd finished and given three cheers, Daniel blew out the candles and made a wish.

'What did you wish for, Daniel?' asked Grandpa Bob.

'I can't tell anyone – not even you, Grandpa – or it won't come true, will it, Daddy?'

Benedict confirmed that this was indeed the case and started to divide up the cake. He made sure that Daniel got the piece in the middle with the crater and the space lion, and that every other child got a slice with either an alien or a spaceship on it. The remainder, he shared between the adults. There was at least a five-minute silence while everyone munched.

'It's a wonderful cake, Stella,' said Catherine. 'Delicious and light as air.'

'And decorated with one arm tied behind your back, or so I hear,' added Grandpa Bob.

'Well, not quite as bad as all that.' Stella smiled gratefully at these two unexpected allies.

Once the cake was finished, the adults began clearing the table and the children sat on the lawn to play pass the parcel. Benedict rigged the game to make sure that the music stopped on a different child each time so everyone got a little gift – wooden yo-yos, which had Miranda's name written all over them. By the time the table was cleared, Benedict had moved onto musical statues and insisted that all the adults join in as well. To give the children a fair chance, adults under fifty had to stand on one leg when the music stopped.

Stella joined in, but when the music stopped, she wobbled about precariously. It had been a bad idea to wear heels to a garden party.

'Out, Stella,' announced Benedict. 'You're out. You're moving all over the place, and you're nothing like a statue at all.'

Stella, pretending to sulk, clomped off to sit down. The children were all trying to stay still, but eventually Daniel burst out laughing and wobbled over.

'Daniel's out too. Off you go, son. Anyone else? No? Right then. On with the music.'

Daniel sat next to Stella while the game continued. He linked her good arm.

'Thank you for my lovely cake. Did you bake it yourself? You're very clever. My Daddy knows about science things, but you know about cleverer things, don't you, like broccoli biscuits and alien cakes and brilliant presents. I hope you never go home. Can you come and live here, please?'

Stella bit her lip and was struggling to find the right words when she was spared from answering by the arrival of a man dressed in a silver cape and top hat riding up the garden path on a blue bicycle that was far too small for him.

Daniel jumped up and shouted, 'It's a magician. Look, everyone, it's a magician!'

The magician doffed his top hat, flicked back his cape, and produced a bouquet of flowers, which he presented to Stella, much to her surprise. One of Nasty Nigel's sons pointed at the new arrival.

'You're too big for that bike, mister. It's for a little kid.'

The magician rubbed his chin and pondered for a while. Without speaking, he looked around the garden, examining each child in turn until his eye fell on Daniel. Then he beckoned him over and presented the bicycle to him. Daniel's mouth opened in a big O as he took possession.

'Daddy, is this for me? My very own bike with only two wheels on it?'

Benedict nodded and Daniel passed the bike to Stella before rushing over to hug his father and say thank you. The magician rummaged in his wide sleeves, and after a prolonged search, revealed a telescope, which he also presented to Daniel.

'Daddy, is this off you as well? A proper grown-up telescope?'

'It's from your aunt. Go and say thank you.'

Daniel ran to Miranda and kissed her, then she extracted the telescope from him and carried it into the house, no doubt to put it somewhere it wouldn't get broken. The magician then proceeded to work his way through the children. First rolling up his sleeves to prove there was nothing there, he produced a series of bubble blowers from behind each child's left ear. He did his whole act without speaking, and the children were fascinated by him, especially when he put Nasty Nigel behind the garden shed and made him disappear. Stella wondered if she was the only audience member who wished he wouldn't come back. Sadly, Nigel emerged from the kitchen only moments later and crept up rather too close behind her.

'It's not real, you know,' he said. 'It's just make-believe.'

'Obviously,' she whispered, 'but the kids love magic, so try not to spoil their fun.'

'I wasn't talking about the magician's act. I was referring to all that astrology rubbish. I can't believe Benedict's allowed you to fill his son's head with all that dangerous made-up stuff.'

'What?' Stella whipped round to stare at him. 'There's nothing dangerous about it at all. I was only teaching Daniel the zodiac, and there's no harm in that.'

'There's plenty of harm in that when the child on the receiving end is the son of one of the country's leading astronomers. Have you any idea how ridiculous you've made Benedict look in front of everyone?'

'What, in front of a bunch of little kids and their parents at a Sunday-afternoon tea-party?'

'These parents aren't just any old people. They're part of the academic community, and it's a tight-knit one. What do you think the chances of Benedict being taken seriously for major government grants are, when he has a girlfriend whose head's filled with superstitious nonsense?'

Stella was too angry to speak. Nigel's words were like poison, and she struggled to understand how someone who barely knew her could apparently hate her so much.

'Nigel, you're being very unfair,' she said, 'and a child's birthday party is hardly the place for this discussion.'

'Unfair? I'll tell you what's unfair. A man who has worked for over a decade to build the reputation of his department to the extent that he's even in the bidding for a grant like this. Then to lose it all because of some muddle-headed stargazer who's hooked him in under false pretences. And he will lose the grant, because these awards are always governed by reputation and standing, and thanks to you, missy, he'll lose those too.'

Tears stung Stella's eyes as she fled from the garden, determined not to cause a scene.

Chapter Fourteen

Stella escaped to the bathroom and locked the door behind her. In the mirror, her chin dimpled with the effort of not crying. She couldn't believe she'd let that awful man say those things about her. And as for saying those things about astrology, it was a direct insult to her mother. She hated herself for not standing her ground and defending her beliefs, but it would take more than a horrible man like Nigel for her to make a scene at a children's party. She rinsed her face with cold water and looked at herself in the mirror. A bit red-eyed, but if she waited a while, the redness would fade. As she dried her face, there was a tap at the door.

'Stella, are you in there?'

'Yes. Sorry, won't be long.'

'Open up and let me in, will you?'

Stella, recognising Catherine's gentle tones, opened the door and let her in. The older woman took one look at her and pressed her lips together.

'I knew it,' she said. 'What did that awful man say to you?'

'Nothing, really. I'm just being over-sensitive.'

Catherine sat on the edge of the bath and patted it, so Stella sat down beside her.

'You're not being over-sensitive. I heard him hissing away at you like a cobra. I couldn't hear what was being said, but the venom was fairly spraying out of him. Then you dashed off and I just wanted to check you were all right. Benedict's so tied up with the children, he didn't notice what was going on.'

'You're too sweet, Catherine. Especially when, you know...' Stella trailed off, unable to find the words to talk about this kind woman's daughter.

'It's all right, Stella, I do know what you mean.' She sighed. 'It's been so hard without Anna. For Benedict, for Daniel, for all of us. We miss her terribly, and we always will.'

Stella noticed a tear shining in the older woman's eye and patted her hand.

'But the thing is, life goes on. My Anna loved life and she wouldn't want Benedict and Daniel pining away forever. She'd want them to be happy, and that means finding love with someone.'

'Ooh, I don't know about love. I mean, we hardly know each other. We've only met a few times, and I'm moving to Canada soon, but they're bound to find someone. The right person.'

'Yes, I'm sure they will.' Catherine looked at Stella as if weighing something up in her mind. 'Come back down with me. Put a brave face on and don't let that pompous swine think he's got one over on you.'

They walked downstairs together, and Stella fixed a cheerful expression on her face before going back out into the garden. It slipped slightly when she saw Nigel and Benedict in a conspiratorial huddle. As she drew near, they both stopped talking and looked up.

'Stella,' said Benedict. 'Wondered where you'd got to. I was asking Nigel what he'd said to frighten you away.'

'Just sorting out my splint.' Stella, cheered by the

138

presence of Catherine, looked her enemy in the eye. 'It'll take more than Nigel to frighten me away.'

'Glad to hear it. The magician's just left, so Daniel's going to open his other presents now.'

Daniel sat with his guests, who helped him to unwrap an assortment of scientific toys, which included the very same orrery that Stella had almost bought from the museum shop. When she saw it was from Nigel, she was doubly relieved that she'd changed her mind at the last minute.

While Benedict picked up the wrapping paper, Miranda fetched out the party bags. Daniel was the perfect little host, presenting each child with a parting gift and thanking them for coming. The guests gathered up their belongings and started to leave, and Daniel, assisted by Grandpa Bob's hand on the saddle, wobbled his way to the end of the drive on his new bicycle to wave goodbye. When his friends and their parents had gone, Daniel's grandparents continued helping him to practise riding his bike. Just as he was beginning to gain his balance, Miranda announced that she was also leaving.

'Thank you for coming to my party, and for my telescope, Aunty Miranda.'

'You're most welcome, Daniel. I've had a lovely time, and you'll see me next weekend while your dad's away working. Goodbye, darling.'

She knelt to kiss him and then stood up. 'Goodbye, Bob and Catherine. It was wonderful to see you again.' She kissed each of them in turn and shook Stella's hand, wishing her a safe journey home. With a final smile at Daniel, she climbed onto her own bike and pedalled away.

As everyone came back up the drive, Stella told Benedict that she was going to get ready for the station.

'You know,' he said, frowning at her wrist. 'I doubt you can manage on the train with your luggage and only one active arm.'

'There's just my rucksack and a bunch of flowers, so it'll be fine.'

'I don't think it will be fine. Let me drive you home. Daniel's going to be awake late so we could have something to eat first and then I could drop you off afterwards.'

'Thanks, but it'll make it too late a night for Daniel. I'll be fine, honestly.'

'Nonsense,' Catherine chimed in. 'Benedict, you go to London with Stella and leave Daniel here with us. We spend so little time with him, it would be lovely to have him to ourselves, and as we're staying over in any case, there's no need to hurry back.'

'Kind of you both to offer, but it's his birthday, and… you know, I should stay with him on this day of all days, and with you two.'

Catherine sat down on a deck chair, fixed Benedict with a look and shook her head.

'Daniel,' she called out, 'how would you like to spend the evening with Grandma and Grandpa? We'll take you out for tea somewhere. What do you say?'

'Ooh, can I, Daddy? Please say yes.'

Benedict looked steadily back at Catherine and gave in gracefully. 'All right then, son. It looks like I've been outmanoeuvred.'

'Really,' protested Stella, 'I don't want you all going to so much trouble on my account.'

'Not another word,' said Catherine, 'or we'll be terribly offended. Off you go, and we'll sort ourselves out here, won't we, my favourite grandson?'

'Grandma, I'm your only grandson.' Daniel hopped onto his grandmother's lap to discuss where to go for tea.

Stella, still feeling guilty about the whole idea, went off to pack.

After lots of goodbyes, Daniel swung on the gate while his grandparents stood behind him, waving. Now that Benedict and Stella were out of the easy warmth of the garden and alone in the car, the atmosphere was strained. Judging by his profile, Benedict was tense. His jaw was clenched and his knuckles were white, even though they were only trickling along in light Sunday-afternoon traffic. Clearly, he was irked about something but it was hard to know what. Since it had been his idea to drive her home, it clearly wasn't that, but his initial suggestion had included his son. It certainly hadn't been his idea to leave Daniel behind and have dinner alone with her, so maybe that was the problem – it was his son's birthday after all. On top of that, seeing Bob and Catherine must have stirred up feelings about his wife and today's terrible anniversary. Unable to bear silence all the way to London, she cleared her throat and decided to break it.

'Well, everyone enjoyed the party and Daniel had a great time.'

Benedict continued to stare straight ahead. 'Yes, he did.'

'And the magician went down a storm. Thanks for the bouquet, by the way. That was a thoughtful touch.'

'Nothing to do with me. Something the magician does at every party, I imagine.'

Immediately, all the colour and perfume drained from the flowers. Stupidly, she'd thought Benedict had meant them for her, when they were nothing more than a routine party trick. The magician was probably booked months ago, long before Stella was on the scene, so the flowers were likely destined for Miranda or Catherine, had they been closer to hand.

They sat in silence all along the country roads, and Stella watched the green hedgerows whizzing past. She wondered if she could just roll from the car on the next slow bend and hitch a ride to London. Even with a sprained wrist, it was tempting to take the risk as the atmosphere in the small car was bordering on painful. But once they joined the M40, Benedict eased his grip on the wheel and his jaw relaxed by at least one millimetre.

'What did you make of Nigel on making his acquaintance for the third time?'

'Nigel? He's very… forthright isn't he?'

'That's one way of describing him. Did he upset you?'

'No,' she lied. 'Well, maybe a bit.'

'Sorry about that. My fault for leaving you to his not-so-tender mercies, but I do wish you'd notified me that you're an astrologer.'

'Notified? Sorry, but I didn't realise there was a form to fill out. Would you like to see my passport as well?'

'No, of course not. But I thought you were a flat-sitter.'

'I am. Flat-sitting is how I keep a roof over my head – many roofs over my head, I should say – but it doesn't pay anything. Astrology is how I earn my crust, and besides that, it's my passion in life.'

'Well, I just wish you hadn't kept it from me.'

'I didn't keep it from you.' Her faced warmed at this fib. 'It just never came up. Anyway, I thought you'd have guessed.'

'Foolishly perhaps, considering we met at an *astronomy* lecture, I assumed you had an interest in astronomy.'

'I do have an interest in astronomy, but only to help with my astrology.'

He fell silent again while he pulled into the fast lane to overtake a line of trucks moving slowly up a long incline and for a while they were jammed between articulated lorries and the central reservation. The small car was noisy and low to the ground, so it felt as though they were going a lot faster than the sixty-nine miles per hour they were actually doing. The lorry driver at the front of the queue flashed Benedict back in and he thanked the driver with a brief lift of his left hand.

'Stella, you don't really believe in all that stuff, do you?'

'I do believe in all that *stuff*, as you put it. And if you and your astronomer friends would be more open-minded, you'd know that the ancients only developed astronomy to improve their understanding of astrology, so it was no more than a means to an end.'

Even though Benedict was no longer in the middle of

142

overtaking, he fell quiet again, and the white knuckles were back.

'Stella, I don't want to upset you, but it's difficult to comprehend how anyone sane can believe in this … I don't know… hocus-pocus.'

'Hocus-pocus? Now you sound just like Nigel. And here was me thinking you were a scientist. Aren't you lot meant to keep an open mind?'

'Yes, but not so open that wool can gather.'

'Are you calling me a wool-gatherer?'

'No, it's just–'

'Because I had enough of remarks like that at school, and just because I only have a handful of ropey GCSEs instead of a swanky doctorate doesn't mean you get to insult my intelligence.'

She turned away from him and stared at the passing hedgerows again. Snide comments were something she was well accustomed to, but not generally from someone she liked. Benedict was treading on dangerous territory. While Stella didn't want to have a row on the motorway, she wasn't going to take these insults twice in one afternoon. She'd never forgive herself for not standing up for her mother's teachings.

'I'm sorry,' he said, eventually. 'I didn't mean to insult you.'

But. There was definitely a but coming. She could feel it in her water.

'But it doesn't matter whether I believe in astrology or not, it's just very difficult for me in my position. You must understand that.'

'Yes, your friend Nigel was only too keen to tell me all the intricate details of your precious grant applications and how I was the greatest threat to astronomy since they jailed Galileo. Well, I'd hate to get in the way of your work, so you can drop me off at the nearest garage or station or whatever, and I'll take a cab from there.'

'I absolutely will not drop you off at a station, let alone a garage. I'm taking you home, whether you like it or not. Stella, I didn't mean to hurt your feelings. It's just that people like Nigel are so traditionally minded. There's such fierce competition for grants, and reputation counts as much as academic ability. I didn't make the system, but I have to work within it.'

'No need to explain yourself to me. Drop me off, and we'll call it a day. You can write me off as a visiting eccentric you once had the misfortune of being taken in by. I'm sure your astronomy mates will forgive you once they know there's a few thousand miles between us.'

Her voice was wobbling so she said no more. What an awful finish to the weekend. Why hadn't Nasty Nigel just kept his big mouth shut? But it wasn't really Nigel's fault – he was just the messenger, however unpleasant – it was mainly Benedict's fault for being such an insufferable snob. And while that part was also true, Stella knew she had to bear some responsibility. Benedict was right, and she should have mentioned her interest in astrology earlier. There was always going to be some ribbing, and she was used to that, but she hadn't expected to be accused of something as ruinous as this, as if she'd deliberately set out to wreck a man's career and destroy the reputation of his college.

Well, she wouldn't make a mistake like this again. In the unlikely event she let another man within six feet of her, she'd introduce herself as Stella McElhone, jobbing astrologer and incidental flat-sitter. Maybe she should get some business cards made.

Her breath had fogged up the side window and before she realised what she was doing, she'd drawn the glyph for Leo with her pinkie. She decided not to rub it out. Next time Benedict was in the car and the side window misted up, it would reappear. That would show him. Really, her trip to Canada could not come soon enough so she could move on with her life and forget all about this prejudiced, narrow-minded elitist.

They were at Notting Hill now, so providing they didn't

get lost, she'd be home in quarter of an hour and then it would all be over, bar the ice cream. There was still the best part of a tub in the freezer from the last time he'd upset her. From when she'd allowed herself to be upset by him, she corrected herself. Well, no more. As they passed Lord's cricket ground, she put her hand on her seat-belt so she'd be ready to release it the second he pulled up. They arrived outside Stella's apartment block without getting lost once, she noted miserably, and when Benedict switched off the engine, he took her good hand.

'Please look at me, Stella. Perhaps the timing just wasn't right for us. I do hope you can forgive me?'

'There's nothing to forgive. Please pass on my regards to Bob and Catherine, who seem like lovely people. I'm going to miss Daniel. You will tell him I said goodbye, won't you?'

'I will. He'll miss you, and if I'm completely honest, I'll miss you as well.'

'I'm sure your multi-million-pound grant will soon take the sting out of it. Open the boot, please, so I can get my things.'

With that, she got out of the car and tugged at the boot, which didn't open. No central locking, of course. Benedict also got out, opened the lock with a key and took out her rucksack and the flowers.

'Let me carry them up to your flat for you. I can at least be that civil.'

'No need. I can manage by myself, thank you.'

'Why do you insist on being so stubborn? Do you want to hurt your wrist even more?'

Stubborn? Benedict Redman was a fine one to talk. She huffed and stalked towards the door, key at the ready. Ernie the porter looked up and smiled.

'Evening, Stella,' he said. 'You been in the wars, mate?'

'Evening, Ernie. It certainly feels that way.'

Ernie gave a curt nod to Benedict and watched them head for the lift, where they waited in silence – a silence that continued as the lift travelled up to her floor. Stella opened the door to her flat and turned on the light. Benedict followed her in and put her bag and the ill-gotten flowers on the table. He paused, close to her. Stella didn't know what she wanted more: to cry, to kiss him or to shove him out of the door and never see him again. Instead, she did nothing, but merely stood there, looking at the floor.

'Well, if that's everything,' he said, 'I'd best be off.'

'Yes, you'd best. Thanks for the lift.'

'It's nothing. Thanks for everything you did for Daniel's birthday. You really made his day.'

Stella did not raise her head. Her eyes were stinging with tears and she couldn't bear to look at him. Benedict leaned forwards and tried to kiss her on the cheek, but the contact was more than she could stand and she pulled away so his lips brushed only the air next to her face.

'Bye, Benedict,' she said with her back to him.

'Goodbye, Stella.'

Without another word, he walked to the door, clicking it shut behind him. Stella couldn't believe that he'd actually gone. Quickly, she turned out the light and peered down at the street to where his stupid little yellow car was waiting for him. A few moments later, Benedict walked out of the building and got into his car without so much as a glance up at her window, then drove off in the wrong direction. She wiped her eyes on her sleeve. No point crying over him. He'd gone for good, and just as well.

Chapter Fifteen

Stella woke early, pulled the bed-clothes up to her chin and closed her eyes to shut out the morning for a while longer. Despite her best efforts, she was wide awake with her mind whirling, and hiding in bed would change nothing, so she pushed back the covers and got out of bed.

'No more,' she told herself in the bathroom mirror. 'Benedict Redman – sorry, Professor Benedict Redman – is a pompous, insecure bigot, and I want nothing more to do with him.'

Perhaps unfair, but she wanted to clear this man from her mind, so she wasn't going to permit any pleasant thoughts about him, and she would not allow herself to think of little Daniel at all. It was idiotic getting so attached to people she hardly knew.

She had no client appointments until early evening, so to help blot the bigot from her mind, she'd have a day out, and she'd do her very best to do something astrology-related, something that would honour her beliefs and her mother's legacy – ideally something that would stick it to Professor Redman.

She showered and dressed in her favourite jeans and a white linen shirt. After slipping a wide silver bangle onto her

147

arm, she brushed her hair until it shone. She looked pale and drawn, but she'd live. While she breakfasted on toast and coffee, she checked her phone for ideas. In Covent Garden, there was a quaint emporium selling mystical paraphernalia, so she decided to treat herself and maybe spend some time around people who didn't think she was a half-wit.

During the Tube journey, she tried hard not to think of Benedict. If only she wasn't contracted to flat-sit in London for a while yet, she could take herself to the other end of the country, or to another country, come to that. Anywhere far away from Oxford. She considered contacting the flat-sitting agency to see if she could break the contract but soon rejected that idea. Breaking her current contract half-way through would cost a serious number of reputation points, which would put the Canada assignment at risk, and she'd also have to go back to getting bookings for grungy flats in out-of-the-way locations with only one or two nights at a go. That was where she'd started out all those years ago, and she had no desire to return to that insecure lifestyle. Canada was not too far off, so she'd just have to wait it out.

When she got off the train, the station was busy, so she ignored the crowded tin-can lifts and ran up the spiral stairs – all one-hundred-and-ninety-three of them. She swiped her phone at the barrier, and it opened to let her out into the winding streets and quirky shops of Covent Garden. Perhaps in a nod to its flower-market origins, everywhere was decorated with barrows, barrels, baskets and buckets of flowers – even the walls were planted in places – so the streets were bright and fragrant.

While she'd been underground, it must have rained, but the sun had come back out and the wet cobbled streets shone in the summer sunshine. She breathed in the sights and sounds of London hurrying past – serious types in sharp suits, tattooed kids with gravity-defying haircuts, and a jumble of colourful street entertainers. A mime artist, painted to look as though he was made of iron, proffered a bunch of metal flowers and she dropped a pound coin into his hat, remembering the magician at Daniel's birthday party. She had to stop seeing these reminders in everything she saw, because that was no way to move on with her life. Filled with renewed purpose, she set off again, pausing only to window-shop in the pretty pastel-coloured boutiques to either side of her.

It didn't take too long to find the purveyor of mystical supplies, with its lilac shopfront and heavenly incense wafting from the door. The soul-calming effects drew her inside where the air was suffused with a tinkling blend that was part harp and part waterfall. Not an inch of space was wasted and the shop was brim-full of glass cabinets and racks holding crystals, essential oils, tarot cards, crystal balls, candles, scarves and altar accessories. Even the ceiling space wasn't wasted and from high hooks dangled dream-catchers and wind-chimes galore. In short, this little shop contained all the trappings needed for anyone leaning towards a spiritual life and it was the perfect antidote to all the intolerance she'd experienced over the weekend.

The day was young, and she settled in for a good browse, deciding to begin with the bookshelves. After a good look around, she settled on a new book about the Saturn return, which she was excited to read. Really, it would make more sense to buy an e-book so she didn't have to lug it around with her, but she preferred her reference books to be on paper so she could pore over diagrams, highlight them and add in charts and calculations of her own.

On her way to the cashier to pay, a huge amethyst geode caught her eye and she bent down to place her good hand on it. The impulse to buy the purple crystal was strong, but it was over a foot high and she soon talked herself out of it. Apart from the cost, it would be ridiculous to encumber herself with something so big and heavy, even assuming she could lug it home. Her life consisted of living out of a couple of bags and there was no room for excess baggage of any sort.

Sensing a presence at her elbow, she withdrew her hand from the amethyst, remembering the many times she and the other kids from the home had been told by local shopkeepers to look with their eyes and not with their fingers. An elderly lady stood next to her. Frail-looking and barely reaching Stella's shoulder, she had shining white hair feathered around an elfin face. Her sparkling eyes looked almost violet and she twinkled up at Stella. It was as if an amethyst sprite had materialised at her side.

'Oh, that one's not for sale, my love. She is a beauty, though.' The woman pointed at Stella's sprained wrist. 'Do you mind?'

Stella nodded in mute agreement, not entirely sure what she was agreeing to. The woman grasped her injured wrist between both hands and Stella braced herself for pain, but it never came. The woman closed her eyes and began to breathe sharply, deeply and rapidly, until Stella feared she might hyperventilate. The elfin woman nodded with every breath taken, and it appeared she was counting. Warmth surged up Stella's arm, radiating to her chest and filling her with a deep joy that made her forget that she was standing in a shop in central London, holding hands with a complete stranger. When the woman stopped counting, she gently released Stella's wrist and opened her eyes. Stella was puzzled to see that the woman's eyes had lost their purple hue and were just a watery-looking blue, after all. Must have been a trick of the light, or something to do with the sun reflecting off the wet pavements and the shop's colourful façade.

'You'll find that will help to mend your arm more quickly,' said the woman. 'I've also started the healing of the real pain that is in your heart, but it can only truly mend if you learn to accept and let go of those you've lost. Love them by all means, but let them go. It's long past time. Expose yourself to new love, even if it hurts, because you need to trust in life and open your heart again.'

The woman touched her gently on the shoulder and left

the shop before Stella could reply. Her arm and chest were still warm and there was also a patch of warmth on her shoulder where the woman had touched her before leaving. Seeing her dazed expression, the shopkeeper stepped away from the till.

'You've just been Meredithed!'

'I've been what-ithed?'

'Meredithed. That lady just now was Meredith. She's been coming here since forever. Never ever buys anything; just comes in, finds someone in pain and heals them. You're very lucky. She has a high hit-rate according to those who've been on the receiving end. Bit of a legend around here. Some people say she's psychic and that it's not the outer pain she's healing, but something deeper that can't be seen.'

'My arm, well it does feel warm, much warmer than before she touched it at any rate.' And inside her chest, too, but that was harder to explain. 'Anyhow, I'm going to take this book, please, and a much smaller version of that amethyst geode, if you have one.'

Beside the till were arrays of baskets filled with crystals and gemstones. The shopkeeper soon found a suitable pocket-sized crystal cluster and helped Stella to get the amethyst and the book on Saturn into her backpack.

'Will there be anything else? We've got tarot readings upstairs, if you're interested?'

'Ah, no thanks. Not just now. But there is something that you might be able to help me with.'

Stella had enjoyed her shopping trip greatly but still craved the company of her fellow astrologers, so she asked the woman if she was aware of any groups due to meet in the area. The woman pulled a well-used notebook from behind the till.

'Now, I can't guarantee they'll be there, what with it being the summer hols and all, but the Constellations meet on the second Thursday night of the month if memory serves.'

The Constellations? It sounded like some kind of retro

eighties band. The shopkeeper flicked through the book until she reached a page with dozens of crossings out and additions. 'They come and go, these groups, but here we are. Yes, second Thursday, which is this week by my count.' She tapped the page with a silver-ringed index finger. 'There, that's the pub in Chelsea where they meet. Seven onwards…'

'And you're certain they're astrologers and not astronomers?'

'Astronomers? Don't make me laugh. No astronomer would dare darken the door for fear of being slung out on their ear.' She shook her head, smiling. 'Astronomers. What are you like, girl?'

That Thursday night, Stella found herself in a cosy pub in Chelsea, just off the King's Road, chatting with a group of astrologers. They were a close-knit group that had been running for decades, but they welcomed occasional visitors. It was a relief being in the company of like-minded individuals and able to talk about the meaning of various planetary transits without anyone raising an eyebrow or snorting in contempt.

Stella opted for a Belgian beer that had been brewed in a Trappist monastery for almost two centuries because she rather liked its romantic history. Liquid bread, they called it, and those monks certainly knew a thing or two about brewing as she was now well into her second pint. Malty, with a floral tang, it didn't taste especially strong, but her face felt hot and she was getting a bit giddy, so it must be stronger than it looked. She peered at the beer board, which stated that her liquid bread was just shy of ten percent ABV – whatever ABV was – so it was about the same as prosecco. But when had she ever drank fizz by the pint? Time to slow down.

Her nearest neighbour was a man called Jim, who was

very good looking, with green eyes that were almost hypnotic. He was holding the floor with his views on the meaning of the current challenging angle between Saturn and Pluto.

'This aspect is affecting everyone in some way. It's all about loss and fear of loss, of feeling constrained and held back in some way,' he said, sweeping his long, dark hair back from his face with his left hand. 'If we all looked deeply into our lives, we'd see the truth of that motif. Stella, as our honoured guest, have you anything to say on the topic of Cronus?'

By using the Greek name for Saturn, this Jim was testing her mettle, and his eyes glittered as he looked at her. Finding his gaze too intense, she hid behind her beer glass, but he didn't waver and was clearly waiting for an answer, so she was forced to respond.

'Emm, I'm very interested in Shaturn and its vanishing rings,' she said, mortified at slurring her words. Hopefully no one else had noticed, but to avoid a repeat performance, she put down her glass and pushed it away from her.

'*Shaturn's* rings,' said Jim. 'As astrologers, we're not so interested in the physical qualities of the planets. Operating as we do on a symbolic plane, I doubt their apparent fading away is of much importance, so it's hard to say. And to be honest, they fade and come back on a regular basis so it's just an optical illusion.'

Jeery Jim's dismissive tone could almost give Nasty Nigel a run for his money. Stella didn't like the way this man was glowering at her, so she was determined to stand her ground.

'But if...' Deep breath. 'But if *Saturn's* physical rings represent life's boundaries, then their fading must have some symbolic meaning for our lives.' Why, oh why had she got embroiled in this? Really deep breath. 'And quite apart from their regular apparent vanishing and returning, the rings really are vanishing for good now, as they're being absorbed into the planet. Only very recently, I heard an astronomer say–'

'Well if an astronomer says anything, it must be right then.' Jim laughed a rather harsh laugh and the others joined him.

'But it is happening.' Stella's voice rose to a squeak. 'And, it must have some symbolic meaning.'

'You shouldn't place too much store in astronomers. That lot will play anything up if there's a whiff of a grant in the offing. They'd sell their grannies for the price of a new telescope.'

Stella frowned and almost went back to her beer. She knew only too well how much grants mattered to astronomers, but then they were scientists, who needed money for research and discovery, and she felt more than a little insulted on Benedict's behalf. Hearing the snide comments tonight was enough to convince her that astrologers and astronomers were as bad as each other sometimes.

Although she couldn't yet see the bottom of her second glass, Stella was light-headed and no longer trusted herself to keep her thoughts to herself. She thanked the group for welcoming her but said she needed an early night and left them to it. As she walked towards Sloane Square station, she heard footsteps hurrying behind her. Hugging her jacket tightly to herself, she walked faster, then whirled round as she felt a tap on her shoulder. It was Jim, who'd followed her from the pub.

'Sorry,' he said. 'I didn't mean to scare you.'

'You didn't scare me,' she lied.

'Good. Look, I didn't mean to upset you back there in the pub. I was having a go at astronomers, not having a dig at you.'

'No worries, honestly. I'm just done in and need an early night, that's all.'

'Well, I wondered whether you'd maybe like to get

together sometime for a drink or a meal. We don't have to argue about Shaturn...'

Stella was tempted for about one second, but seeing his glittering eyes and mocking mouth, she thought instead of Benedict and his crinkled eyes and good-natured smile. Although there was no hope in that direction, she still felt a curious loyalty to him. It would feel wrong to go off with someone else, and it would feel like an even bigger betrayal to go off with someone who had such a dim view of astronomers, even if she did share that dim view. She shook her head.

'It's not a good time for me at the moment, but thank you. Anyway, I need to get going. Goodnight.'

Her rejected would-be suitor merely shrugged and loped back to the pub, not remotely devastated by her refusal. Easy come, easy go, she supposed and continued walking to Sloane Square. She got onto the Tube and sat down, feeling slightly the worse for wear, even though she'd left most of her second drink. Beer and men, she decided, were probably no good for her and best avoided. The rhythm of the train was too lulling and she didn't want to nod off and miss her change at Westminster so she stood up and perched near the door.

When the train pulled into St John's Wood, her head had cleared a little but she was taking no chances and stood on the escalator instead of running up it. On her way towards Abbey Road, she admired the crescent moon. She'd have been better off living thousands of years ago when astrologers and astronomers were one and the same, with the whole point of astronomy being to plot planetary movements to inform astrology and help the ancients to plant and sow, to reap and harvest, to heal both the body and the spirit. Perhaps the two disciplines were destined to move further and further away from their original starting point when the ancients, who were more holistic in their approach, saw the beauty and truth in both elements of their stargazing. Times had changed though, and astrology and astronomy had split apart, and would probably always be split apart. Just like her and Benedict.

Outside her apartment block, she struggled to get her key in the front door and to her consternation, Ernie came to open it for her.

'Neither of your hands working this evening, Stella?' he asked with a wink. 'And no wonder, when you smell like a brewery.'

'Thank you, Ernie. Sorry for making you get up. And you're right about the brewery.'

'No need to apologise to me. I used to love the odd pint, but I've no head for beer these days. You'll have a sore one in the morning, I expect.'

'A well-deserved sore head, Ernie. Courtesy of an order of Trappist monks in Belgium.'

'Oh, you don't do things by halves, do you? Get a pint of water down you, mate. Goodnight then and God bless.'

Stella smiled and bid Ernie goodnight, trying not to weave as she walked to the lift. Best not to even attempt the stairs.

It was easier to unlock the door to her flat, and after she'd locked it behind her, she made some coffee and sat out on her balcony, watching the traffic pause at the famous zebra crossing outside her window. She tried to imagine the Beatles walking over the crossing, and wondered if the Fab Four had realised when they did it that they would spawn thousands of tourists, decades later, from all over the world, who would try to recreate the scene. Ernie was always telling anyone who'd listen that the fans were posing on the wrong zebra crossing, but he was usually ignored.

Chapter Sixteen

In the morning, Stella was grateful that it was time to get up, even though her head felt as if she'd not slept at all. Judging by the snatches of dreams that kept coming back to her, she suspected that the strong beer and her mind were working together to sort through some of the events of the past few days. Although she didn't have a headache as such, she was groggy and hoped a bath would put her right.

She slid into lavender bubbles up to her neck and propped her bad arm on the side of the bath, wrapped in a carrier bag. Her plan was to steep for as long as it took for the hot water and lavender to do their job. With nothing else to occupy her mind, it was impossible not to think back to the bath that Benedict had run for her, scattered with rose petals from his garden. A rose-filled bath. Now was that really the work of someone who wanted to be just friends? Then there was the near-miss kiss, of course. Not something that would occur in a strictly platonic relationship, surely. Stella asked herself for the hundredth time why she couldn't be happy with someone nice and uncomplicated, without ties, emotional baggage and hang-ups about people's beliefs. The only trouble was, there were umpteen men like that around, but Stella hadn't felt anything for any of them. She'd had relationships, and could count them on the fingers of her good hand, but they'd always fizzled out when she lost interest. At this rate, she'd be alone for the rest of her life, which she wasn't entirely unhappy about. No, that wasn't strictly true, but being alone was the safest option for her, and one that meant not having to open herself up to a new world of pain and loss because she'd lost too many people already in her life and didn't want to lose any more. If the price for that safety was being alone, then it was a price worth paying.

Clear-headed and newly resolved, she surfaced from the water and clambered out of the bath. Once dry, she dusted her skin with violet powder to lift her spirits and looked at her wrist splint, wondering how much longer she'd have to put up with it. The hospital in Oxford had made an appointment with a local clinic for a check-up this Saturday, and it couldn't come soon enough. In the meantime, she had a couple of astrology readings booked in during the early evening, so she'd need to produce the charts and spend some time analysing and interpreting them ahead of her video calls with clients. She'd have to type her notes one-handed, which would probably take her at least twice as long as usual, so she'd better get cracking straight after breakfast.

———

By early afternoon, Stella had finished analysing the birth charts and had made a good start on the interpretations, but the one-handed typing was driving her up the wall and she was also famished, which was as good a reason as any to take a break. There wasn't much in the fridge, so unless she wanted beans on toast, she'd have to hit the shops. While debating whether to go shopping or to make do and mend, her phone rang. It was an unknown number. She was about to reject the call but picked up in case it was the clinic calling about her appointment.

'Hello,' she said. 'Stella McElhone here.'

'Hello, Stella,' said a woman's voice on the other end. 'It's Catherine here. Catherine Telford. Daniel Redman's grandmother.'

'Oh, yes. Hello, Catherine. How are you?'

'I'm very well, thank you. And how is your poor arm?'

'On the mend, thanks. I'm off to the doc's at the weekend for a check-up.'

'Well, here's hoping you won't have that splint on for very much longer. It's the wrong time of year to be walking around with such an ugly thing on your arm, especially on such a pretty girl.'

'Catherine… what are you after?'

'All right, you got me. I'm coming up to London on Saturday afternoon and wondered if you'd let me buy you lunch.'

'Ooh, I don't know about that. It's very kind of you to offer, but you know, things are a bit, well… you know.'

'I know exactly how things are, my dear, but I feel bad since we hardly got to say hello before you were suddenly gone again. Go on, just one tiny lunch, with absolutely no strings attached. Besides, you'd be doing me a favour. There's a fabulous little brasserie near you and I can hardly go alone. I'm just not one of those people who can sit on my own with a book.'

'What about Bob? Surely he'd like to go with you.'

'Alternative arrangements. What you don't yet know about me is that I'm a cricket widow. Please say yes to lunch. It would make me very happy.'

Stella thought for a while. On the one hand, seeing Benedict's mother-in-law risked picking the scab off a wound that was still healing, but on the other, she was a lovely woman and it felt unkind to turn her down.

'Stella, are you still there?'

'Sorry, yes. I'm deciding.'

'And have you decided yet?'

'Yes. I will come to lunch with you, but only if we can go halves.'

'You drive a hard bargain. Agreed. Shall we say one o'clock? I'll book a table and text you the details, and we'll meet there on Saturday.'

Saturday was starting to look like a busy day. The appointment at the clinic was at ten in the morning, but that should leave plenty of time to get home and change. If nothing else, she had a pleasant lunch with a kind companion to look forwards to, provided that she wasn't looking forwards to seeing Catherine for the wrong reasons. She made a firm resolution to resist any urge to ask questions about Benedict, beyond those absolutely required for the sake of politeness.

On Saturday morning, Stella got up early and went to the clinic in nearby Maida Vale. She arrived far too early and put in some time walking the canal path, admiring the brightly painted houseboats moored alongside, which explained why the area was known as Little Venice. It struck her as a pleasant way to live and she made a mental note to watch out for future houseboat-sitting opportunities.

Still early for her appointment, she sat in the medical centre waiting room for what felt like an age. There appeared to be no obvious queuing system. Rather, the receptionist called out names seemingly at random and Stella wondered whether the system was based on favouritism or on likely longevity: those who looked like they had a few years left on the clock could afford to sit about a while longer. To take her mind off the queue, she buried herself in the magazines that were piled up everywhere. By the time she'd discovered how to cook a vegan stroganoff and three new ways to part her hair, the receptionist finally called out her name and pointed her down a narrow corridor. Stella knocked on the door and entered the examining room. The doctor smiled sympathetically at the splint.

'I bet you can't wait to be rid of that thing in this heat.'

Stella nodded in agreement and they discussed the weather while the doctor removed the splint. She examined Stella's pale, slightly withered arm.

'It's healed incredibly quickly. One of the many joys of youth.' The doctor went on to provide advice for aftercare: not to overdo it at first, but equally, to stop favouring her good arm.

After thanking the doctor, and mentally thanking Meredith for her psychic healing powers, Stella took her pale arm out into the sunshine to catch some healing rays. It felt strange now that the splint was finally off. On the way home from the clinic, her arm felt light enough to float away and it took a while before it started to feel normal again. She wouldn't be lifting weights with it anytime soon, but at least her arm was on the mend.

Back in the flat, Stella stepped out of the shower. She'd given her sore arm a good scrub to liven it up and daubed on some arnica healing cream that had a refreshing lemon and ginger scent. After a rummage in her wardrobe, she laid out a couple of frocks, finally opting for a white broderie anglaise pinafore, which would be perfect for such a warm day. She dried herself, dressed and slipped her feet into a pair of white sandals. After a quick check in the mirror, she grabbed her bag and headed out into the hot midday sun, relieved that she'd chosen such a light dress. The restaurant was on the high street, just past the Tube station, but she guessed Catherine would most likely take a cab from Paddington, rather than do battle with the Underground.

On the high street, the delicatessens and bodegas bustled with life and Stella slowed down as she neared the restaurant on the corner. It was a red-brick Victorian affair, a former pub by the looks of it, and an old sign announced in ornate gilt script that the building had once been known as The Sir Isaac Newton. She allowed herself a small smile.

How appropriate when the father of gravity was widely reported to have owned a handful of books on astrology, although she was aware that his collection did include at least one tome that refuted astrology. Sir Isaac Newton or no Sir Isaac Newton, Stella worried that this place was going to hurt her pocket. Still, it was only lunch so she'd get away with having just the one course and she'd choose whatever was cheapest on the menu.

Inside, she gave her name to the maître d', who invited her to follow him. The restaurant was sunny and bright, courtesy of a large glass atrium and the sunlight reflecting off the glasses hanging above the bar. She was shown to a table at the far side of the restaurant and was a little disappointed when the maître d' held out a chair for her and she found herself facing the wall with her back to the door. Given the option, she'd have preferred to sit the other way round so she could see Catherine coming in, whereas now she'd have to keep twisting awkwardly if she wanted to see anything. She toyed with the idea of switching places, wondering if it was possible to stand up without making her heavy chair scrape loudly, but she was saved from social ruin when a waiter arrived to take her drinks order.

A tall cylinder of sparkling water with ice and lime soon appeared in front of her, which would give her something to do with her hands until Catherine arrived. Stella was never any good at being in restaurants on her own – she shared that much in common with her lunchtime companion. Pavement cafés were doable as they were designed for watching the world go by, but in the confines of a restaurant, she always felt self-conscious dining alone. Since she spent so much of her life alone, this meant that she very rarely dined out, so today was something of a novelty for her.

Resisting the urge to fiddle with the cutlery, she held her hands together in her lap, wondering whether the quiet restaurant would fill up without her even realising. Maybe the waiter had sat her here so she wouldn't feel stared at by other customers, but it still felt strange. Eventually, she heard the door open, and when she turned around in her seat, she was pleased to see Catherine coming towards her, but was surprised to see Bob holding the door open behind her. She stood up to greet them both and asked Bob what had happened to his cricket match.

'Oh, I've seen the start of play and they've broken for lunch now, so I thought to have a bite with you both here, if you don't mind the imposition.'

'It's no imposition at all and it's lovely to see the pair of you.'

'How's the arm? Good riddance to that splint, I expect?'

'It's fine thanks, Bob. And yes, I'm glad to see the back of the splint.'

'Bob, why don't you get busy with the wine list and choose us a nice crisp white,' said his wife. 'We could use a cold glass of wine on a lovely day like this, couldn't we, Stella?'

'It's a bit early for me...' Seeing Catherine's expression, Stella gave in gracefully, 'but I'll make an exception for you.'

The waiter came, took the wine order and asked if they were ready to order their food. Catherine said they needed more time and shooed him away, and when Bob raised his brows at his wife, she frowned at him. Stella sensed domestic disharmony in the air. Deciding that discretion was definitely the better part of valour, she excused herself to the ladies so they could fight it out between them.

Well away from the zone of conflict, she leaned on the vanity counter and sampled the soap, followed by the hand lotion. Both smelt weirdly good enough to eat. That was probably just her appetite kicking in as breakfast had been ages ago. Another five minutes should be long enough to give the Telfords time to sort themselves out. Was Bob's nose out of joint because he'd been co-opted into having lunch when he'd have preferred to grab a pie and a pint at the cricket ground? He hadn't seemed unhappy when they arrived, but why was he here in the first place? Perhaps

Catherine had changed her mind, deciding she didn't have much to say to Stella, after all, and had fetched her husband along as a buffer zone. Poor man, having to miss his match when he was so near to his beloved cricket ground.

Bob was a lovely man, but Stella was a bit disappointed by his appearance as she'd been hoping that Catherine might share some news of Benedict. Probably just as well he was here, though, otherwise she'd only be tormenting herself with news of what she couldn't have. With a final dab of the lovely hand lotion, she stopped dawdling, knowing she couldn't lurk in the ladies any longer without looking bad-mannered or just plain weird. Hopefully, she'd given Catherine and Bob enough time to get the bickering out of their systems.

When Stella came out of the bathroom, she nodded to the maître d' and returned to her table. Catherine and Bob had obviously not stopped bickering and had taken it outside. In their place, looking quite sheepish, was Benedict. He was wearing a sand-coloured moleskin jacket and one of his lovely sky-blue shirts, open at the neck. Her heart gave an involuntary leap, and she tried not to trip over her own feet as she walked towards him.

It felt like a hundred miles back to the table. Part of her was tempted to turn and run. It would serve him right if she did, for messing her around so much, but one more look at him told her she was going nowhere. When she reached the table, Benedict stood and pulled out her chair. Stella sat woodenly and stared at him with glassy eyes, feeling drunk even though she'd not yet touched a drop of wine. She looked at his pale eyes and the crinkles surrounding them, which told her without looking at his mouth that he was smiling at her.

'Hello, Stella.'

She swallowed and barely managed to croak a reply. Then they fell into silence, which was broken only by the waiter arriving to take their order. They weren't anywhere near ready, but the waiter, who evidently had decades of experience with this sort of thing, had judged the situation perfectly and provided a welcome third-party distraction.

'Thank you,' said Stella, who hadn't looked at the menu yet. 'I'll have a very well-done steak and salad.' It was a brasserie, so they'd be bound to have steak and salad, but so much for choosing the cheapest item on the menu. She'd just have to cut back on her shopping for a week or two.

The waiter paused with his pencil poised above his pad.

'How well done exactly, madam?'

'Oh, about five seconds before the smoke alarm goes off, please.'

'Very good, madam.' The waiter noted the order without so much as a roll of his eyes and Stella admired his restraint.

'And for you, sir?'

'Same, thank you.'

The waiter poured the wine that Catherine had ordered. Benedict raised his glass, but Stella wasn't letting him off the hook that easily.

'What exactly are we toasting, may I ask?'

After a brief pause, Benedict raised his glass again. 'To your arm being back in commission.'

This was pretty disappointing as toasts went. She hadn't been expecting a declaration of undying love or anything, but a toast to her arm bordered on pathetic. She raised her own glass about an inch and forced a half-smile. Taking a large gulp of wine, she decided to be direct.

'Is anyone going to explain to me how I met Catherine for lunch, she turns up with Bob, they start having a domestic, I go to the ladies and when I return there's you?'

'Yes, there's me. I expect you do want an explanation. Where to begin?'

'The beginning isn't a bad place to start.'

Stella's initial delight at seeing Benedict was wearing thin and now she felt mostly cross. A busy restaurant wasn't the time or the place for an emotional outburst though, so she smoothed her dress over her knees and examined the cutwork on the hem for a couple of seconds to calm her down.

'Nice frock, by the way.'

At this, her head jerked up. *Nice frock, by the way?* Honestly, she may as well be passing the time of day with Ernie on her way in and out of the building. Next, he'd be calling her *mate*.

'Mm, thanks a lot. Anyway, back to the beginning.'

'You'll perhaps recall that I was meant to be working away this weekend...'

'Vaguely.' She was able to recall his every planned move in perfect detail, but there was no reason for him to know that.

'Bob had spare tickets for Lord's and asked if we'd like to go. It was a great opportunity to take Daniel to his first proper cricket match...'

'So, you cancelled your work trip. I get that. But would you care to explain why you're here with me and not at Lord's with Daniel?'

'We-ell, I'd arranged to meet Catherine and Bob here for lunch. Afterwards, we were going to go to the cricket ground, and Catherine was going to go shopping.'

'Benedict, does that mean you didn't know I was going to be here?'

'Yes. No.' He looked down at the table. 'That is... no, I didn't know you were going to be here.'

'I see.' This was getting worse by the minute. He was only here under false pretences and was probably counting the seconds until he could escape.

'And you, Stella, how were you snared?'

'Catherine called and asked if we could meet for lunch.'

'She did, did she? And was no part of you suspicious that my mother-in-law wanted to meet you for lunch? Right here on your doorstep when she lives seventy or eighty miles away at a conservative estimate.'

'Why would I be suspicious? I've no idea where she lives,

and people come to London all the time. What, do you think we've been set up by your mother-in-law?'

'There's no *think* about it, Stella. Catherine's never shied away from interfering, but this has to be her finest hour.'

Stella didn't know whether to laugh or cry. 'Do you think Bob was in on it?'

Benedict shrugged. 'He wouldn't have had much choice and probably agreed as he was getting a day at the cricket out of it. In fact, I wouldn't be at all surprised if Daniel was in on it, too.'

Stella looked around the restaurant. 'Was Daniel here?'

'We all were. I arrived with him, but we'd hardly sat down and said hello when he needed the loo. Bob said he'd take him. Then about a minute later, Catherine said she needed to powder her nose. Before I could object, she'd gone, almost at a trot. I was just beginning to wonder if the three of them were all right when you appeared in front of me.'

Stella finally laughed. 'I can promise you something. Catherine is one-hundred percent not powdering her nose because I was hiding in the ladies for almost fifteen minutes trying out the hand-cream and she didn't come past me.'

'Why on earth were you hiding?'

'Your in-laws seemed to be on the verge of a domestic, so I was giving them some space.'

'Giving them some space? Oh, Stella, we've both been well and truly had.'

It was hard knowing whether to be happy or angry at Catherine's plotting. Mainly, Stella just felt sad to learn that Benedict hadn't come here of his own free will.

'Apart from anything,' she said, 'I bet you're pretty cheesed off that your in-laws have kidnapped your son and gone off to the cricket without you.'

'I'll get over it. Besides, I'm somewhat consoled by the fact that Catherine has had to forego a lovely lunch in excellent company. Instead, she's going to be stuck at an all-day cricket match. She absolutely loathes cricket. The thought of her sitting in Lord's all afternoon makes me curiously happy.'

'Professor Redman, I never knew you had such a malevolent streak in you.'

'I bet you never knew my mother-in-law had such a manipulative streak in her.'

'No, and she seemed like such a sweet old lady, too.'

'Don't let her catch you calling her old.'

This made them both smile and they clinked glasses. Stella had barely taken a sip of wine when Benedict waved to someone behind her. She turned around in time to see Daniel run in, followed by his grandparents. Before the trio had crossed the floor, a waiter quickly laid three more places at the table.

Daniel arrived first. 'Daddy! Stella! Grandma and Grandpa took me on an adventure, but I wanted to come back and – oh, Stella, I can see your arm again. Is it better?'

'Much better, Daniel. And how are you?'

'Hungry.'

'Then you'd better come and have something.' Stella patted the chair beside her and the little boy sat down, soon followed by his grandparents.

'All right, son,' said Benedict. 'What do you want to eat?'

Daniel grinned at his father. 'Burgers and fries and orange juice with ice cubes and then some ice cream.'

'Well, let's start with one burger and see how you get on.'

Bob ruffled his grandson's hair. 'Tell you what, old boy, let's leave after the main course and I'll buy you the biggest ice cream we can find at the cricket ground. Will that hit the spot?'

'As long as I can have monkey blood on it, Grandpa.'

'Monkey blood?' said Catherine. 'How utterly grotesque.'

'No, it's delish.' The little boy grinned. 'At my birthday party, Stella asked me if I wanted monkey blood on my ice cream.'

On seeing his grandmother's grimace, Stella explained that this was simply the term for raspberry syrup used by children in the north-east of England, but this explanation didn't seem to reduce her anxiety and Catherine took a good swig of wine from Benedict's glass.

The waiter took the three new orders. With a straight face, he informed the table that as the smoke alarms hadn't yet gone off, the steaks weren't quite ready, which meant all the orders would arrive at the same time so everyone could eat together. While they waited, Benedict offered the wine to his in-laws and Daniel got his large glass of orange juice with ice. He happily fished the ice-cubes from his drink and crunched his way through them, setting everyone else's teeth on edge.

While he crunched, he swung his legs. 'Stella, I've missed you loads. Why haven't you been back to see me?'

'I've missed you too, Daniel. Sorry, I've not been to see you, but things have been a little, uh, well... Anyway, tell me what you've been up to in the school hols.

'I've been learning all about dragons.'

'Oh? Dragon lessons sound very exciting.'

'They are. I've been learning how much dragons like crystals and jewels. They eat them and it helps to keep their fire burning. That's why the babies are born in crystal eggs, so they've got some food to light their fire as soon as they get born. If I'm very good, I think Santa might bring me a baby dragon for Christmas.'

On hearing this news, Benedict's eyes widened, and no wonder. If dogs weren't welcome in the Redman household because of Aunt Miranda, then a baby dragon stood no chance.

'Draw breath, lad,' said Bob, 'or you'll run out of steam.'

Sitting as close to Stella as he could without actually sitting on her knee, Daniel continued to discuss his ambitions concerning his prospective pet.

'Have you picked a name for this baby dragon of yours?'

'Yes, I'm going to call him Rory because of all the roaring he'll do.'

'That's a lovely name, and I can't wait to meet Rory.'

Stella was glad that Catherine, Bob and Daniel had returned. The atmosphere prior to their arrival had been awkward to say the least and it was good to have some light relief and effortless conversation. Catherine was making great play at being innocent of any interfering, behaving as if nothing out of the ordinary had happened, and there was no way that Benedict was going to admonish his mother-in-law in the restaurant, if at all.

When the food came, the table continued to be lively, and it was lovely to feel part of this family again, even if only for an afternoon. Daniel looked to be enjoying it too, acting up to the combined attention of his father, grandparents and Stella. He was being ticked off (although not too energetically) by Catherine for eating with his fork in one hand while his other was tucked around Stella's good arm.

Stella doubted that Benedict and his in-laws were truly happy, because times like these must bring it home to them more than ever that Anna should have been here, central to every person at the table, bar Stella. As soon as she'd had the thought, she pushed it out of her mind, determined to stop torturing herself. It made no sense to waste this precious time worrying about what Benedict and his in-laws might or might not be thinking.

When they neared the end of their meal, there was a slightly heated argument about the bill. Stella wanted to pay for herself, but no one at the table would hear of it, and she was told in no uncertain terms to put her purse away. Benedict wanted to pay for everyone but Catherine insisted that she do the honours as atonement for her wicked deeds. As negotiations became protracted, the waiter approached the table with a small salver bearing a booklet embossed with the name of the restaurant. While Benedict and Catherine continued to fight it out, Bob slipped his credit card to the waiter with impressive sleight of hand. Daniel beamed at his grandfather, and the waiter gave a small but knowing nod as he retreated from the table. When the waiter returned to deliver the receipt, along with some chocolate truffles, Catherine and Benedict finally surfaced, as if from underwater, blinking and trying to catch up with what had gone on. Bob took the receipt and folded it into his wallet, winking at Daniel as he did so.

'Well, me boy, what say we get off to the match?'

'Yes, Grandpa.' Daniel got down from the table. 'Daddy, are you coming? It's a shame Stella can't come as well. I bet she'd love to see the cricket.'

'I'm not so sure about that, son. You go and have a good time with your grandparents.'

'But, Daddy, I can't go home without saying goodbye to Stella. Can I go to her house after the cricket do you think? I've never seen it.'

'I don't know, because it'll be late when you come out of the match.' Benedict glanced at Stella. 'We'll have to see.'

'But, Daddy…'

'No buts. I said we'll have to wait and see.'

Stella looked at the boy's sad little face. His upset was probably more to do with his father not going to the cricket with him, and nothing to do with seeing her flat. Perhaps she should clear the way for him. As they said goodbye to the restaurant staff and headed outside, Stella leaned over to Benedict.

'You should go to the cricket and let Catherine come shopping with me as per our original plans. She doesn't even like cricket–'

'I most certainly do like cricket,' interrupted Catherine. 'And I wouldn't miss an afternoon at Lord's for the world.'

Benedict brushed crumbs from Daniel's clothing and gave him tips on what to watch out for at the match. The boy nodded solemnly at each instruction. It was unbearable allowing a father to sacrifice something as important as his son's first cricket match, and Stella stepped back, drawing Catherine with her.

'You meant well by switching places so Benedict and I get to spend some time together, but separating father and son for Daniel's first match? That's not something I want on my conscience. Please come shopping with me. Let the men go to the cricket this afternoon. I'll arrange to meet Benedict soon, and we'll get this thing sorted, I promise.'

Catherine opened her mouth to object but thought better of it. She touched her son-in-law on the shoulder to get his attention, and when he turned, she passed her ticket to him.

'You need to be there with Daniel today. Orders from above.'

Benedict looked at Stella and mouthed 'thank you'. After brief goodbyes and promises to collect Catherine after the match, the three male generations of Daniel's family left. Stella was acutely aware that she'd probably thrown away the last chance she had to make a go of things with Benedict.

'You did the right thing, my dear,' said Catherine. 'Now, you promised me shopping, so let's get cracking in the West End, shall we?'

Chapter Seventeen

The two women were onto their third boutique when Catherine fell in love with a lemon two-piece in slub silk, sighing as she admired the outfit from several angles. The assistant asked if she'd like to try it on, but Catherine shook her head.

'Something that special would only do for a wedding, and there are none on the horizon, I'm afraid.'

The assistant glanced at Stella's left hand. 'Will madam's daughter not be getting married in the near future?'

A veil cast itself across Catherine's features, and Stella tried to eyeball the assistant, who – perhaps realising her blunder – excused herself and moved on to another customer.

Stella raised her brows at Catherine.

'Sorry. That was a bit unfortunate.'

'You've nothing to be sorry for. I can't expect the world to walk on eggshells for me. Do you know what? I will try that outfit on. Come with me. You can give me your opinion while the saleswoman extracts her foot from her mouth. In any event, I imagine your opinion should be more reliable than someone on commission.'

Stella followed her into the changing room, which was

decorated like a French boudoir, plonked herself down on a damask chair next to an occasional table and helped herself to a golden sugared almond from a crystal bonbonnière. She was onto her fourth when Catherine opened the changing-room door, pirouetted and smoothed the dress across her hips.

'Oh dear, I've said goodbye to my girlish figure – too many cream teas over the years, I suppose.'

'Your figure is just fine and that outfit is perfect on you. The colour brings out your eyes and the longline jacket gives you a great silhouette.'

'You really think so?'

'Yes, I really do think so.'

Catherine's face broke into a broad smile. 'Bob always says the kindest things about my new outfits but he's a bit biased and not always telling the gospel truth.'

'I'm sure Bob is most sincere, and you do look lovely.'

'You know, since I rarely get to London these days, I'm going to treat myself to this.' Catherine did another little twirl in the mirror and admired herself. 'And I'll need a hat, some shoes and a bag while we're about it.'

'Then I hope you're packing some serious plastic. This place is no bargain basement.'

'Well, I'm worth it. And do you know what? If I have the perfect wedding outfit, then I'm sure that the perfect wedding will come along soon enough.'

Catherine was as good as her word, and within a couple of hours the two women were laden with colourful cardboard bags with pretty ribbon handles. When Catherine suggested stopping at a café, Stella gratefully agreed. They collapsed at a table and ordered a pot of tea to share. Stella was keen to keep the conversation away from Benedict, and Catherine appeared equally keen not to have the subject wander round to her plotting attempts, so the conversation remained light and easy. Once they'd finished their tea, Catherine leaned down and rubbed her left leg.

'You know, I can't bear the Tube again in this heat so I'm treating us to a cab back to your flat as long as you don't mind an impromptu visitor?'

'Not at all. I'll go and hail a taxi.'

When Catherine came outside five minutes later, Stella was still standing on the pavement, surrounded by shopping bags, waving haplessly as a parade of black cabs sailed by.

'You may as well go and sit down for a bit as I'm having no luck here.'

But Catherine was having none of it and drew herself up to her full height, walked smartly to the kerb, put two fingers in her mouth and gave an ear-splitting whistle, which magically brought a cab to the kerb. Winking at Stella, she climbed in.

'What? You think once you're over sixty you forget how to whistle?'

'I'm impressed and envious. Whistling's something I've never been able to do.'

'Then you must allow me to teach you some time.'

The cabbie glanced in the rear-view mirror and asked them where to. Stella gave her address and was about to give directions when the cabbie pulled away.

'Forget it, my dear,' said Catherine, 'he'll only be insulted if you give him directions.'

At Stella's puzzled look, Catherine informed her that London cab drivers have to do a test called 'The Knowledge' before they get a licence, and pointed out that the driver probably knew every single street, alley and shortcut in London, and all without the aid of satellite navigation. When the cab pulled up in Abbey Road, Stella gathered their things, hopped out and held the door for Catherine, who paid the cabbie. Ernie saw them coming with their shopping and hurried to open the outer door.

'Thanks very much, Ernie.'

'Good shopping trip, ladies?' he said, pressing the lift button for them.

'Yes, thank you,' said Catherine. 'But we're ready to put our feet up.'

'This your mum, Stella?'

'Ah, no.' Unbelievable. Twice in one day. But how to describe their relationship without the aid of an overhead projector or a flipchart or something?

Fortunately, Catherine beat her to it.

'Friend of the family.'

Stella ushered Catherine into the lift.

'Sorry about that. My fault for not introducing you.'

'Please don't worry. These things happen, and I imagine it's as hard for you as it is for me.'

When Stella let Catherine into her flat, she made a beeline for the sofa.

'I hope you don't mind, but I've been dying to do this all day.' Without further ado, Catherine kicked off her shoes and sank back into the sofa. 'I adore the West End, but it's murder on the old tootsies. The Tube would have finished me off.'

'You stay put, and I'll make us a nice cuppa.'

'You're an angel.'

Stella pottered about in the kitchen while Catherine relaxed. 'I hope coffee mugs will do,' she called through the serving hatch, 'as there aren't any teacups.'

'Mugs are fine. We can fit more tea in them. Come and sit next to me, and while we drink, you can tell me exactly what's troubling you.'

'Who me? Nothing's troubling me. I'm absolutely fine.'

'Stella, my dearest girl, if I know one thing in life it's when two people are weighed down by something. And it's the best thing in the world if you talk about it, you know.'

'I know. But, well… you know.'

'What? I'm Anna's mother and you think it's not right to talk to me about your feelings for Benedict?'

Catherine had put her finger on it. It was incredibly

awkward spending time with this woman, given that Stella was only on the scene because Anna had died. She sat down and looked at her feet for a long time, not knowing quite what to say. Then she felt a warm hand patting hers.

'You can count on my blessing and on Bob's, so there should be nothing standing in your way.'

'That's very gracious of you both, Catherine, and I really appreciate it. But even assuming Benedict does like me, there's the problem of the stars. Well, the planets, to be precise.'

'The planets? Whatever can you mean?'

'You know, what with me being an astrologer and Benedict being an astronomer. He's afraid of risking his professional reputation by associating with me, but it's my work and my passion in life, so I couldn't give it up. Not for anyone.'

Stella's head drooped and even a comforting hug from Catherine didn't help her to straighten up again.

'Benedict Redman is made of sterner stuff than that, and he wouldn't dream of asking you to give up your work…'

Catherine trailed off as Stella's chin began to quiver. She tried to get a grip before she found herself sobbing snottily in the arms of someone she'd known for less than a turn of the moon. Unruffled, Catherine offered her a dainty, lace-edged handkerchief and Stella dabbed her watery eyes before passing the now-damp hanky back.

'It's quite all right, my dear. You hang onto it. Now tell me everything. Leave nothing out. You'll feel better for it, I promise.'

And so Stella told this kind woman how she'd lost her parents when she was just a little girl and how astrology was the last link to her childhood. Astrology was how she earned her living, but more importantly, every time she looked at the stars or made an astrological calculation, it brought her closer to her mother, who'd taught her everything. And this woman understood perfectly, as only someone who has experienced great loss truly could.

'So you see, no matter how much I feel for Benedict and Daniel, I cannot and will not betray my mother's legacy.'

'Stella, my darling girl,' began Catherine. 'Benedict would never ask you to betray your calling, just as you would never ask him to give up his.' She sighed and took Stella's hands between hers. 'If you and my son-in-law would only take a step back, you'd both see that what's keeping you apart is nothing at all to do with a bunch of big rocks millions of miles away. You lost both your parents at a tender age, so it's no wonder that you're scared to love anyone in case you lose them in the same way.' She paused to give Stella a little squeeze. 'Likewise, Benedict is terrified of loving another woman in case he loses her again. My daughter was the world to me, and now she's gone, all that I have left of her are Benedict and Daniel. My daughter would want them to be happy again. I want them to be happy again and can't think of anyone that would make them happier than you.' She got up and walked to the window, gazing down into the street below before going on. 'Stella, I'd give everything twice over to have my daughter back. I miss her every single day of my life and always will. But I've accepted that Anna is gone, and as sad as that makes me, I love Benedict and Daniel, and their happiness means more to me than anything else in the world nowadays. And you are the one person who will make their happiness complete.'

If it were only that easy. 'I'm not even sure how Benedict feels about me. He... well... he did almost kiss me the night before Daniel's birthday.' Stella's heart tightened at the memory. 'But the next day, he was as cool as anyone could be. I assumed he'd made a mistake. And that was that.'

The older woman was quick to assure Stella that he hadn't made a mistake. He'd just realised that he'd found someone who made him happy. And that made him feel guilty. He was afraid of being happy, of betraying Anna's memory, and betraying his in-laws, but Catherine insisted he was doing no such thing, and she and Bob wanted nothing more than for their grandson and his father to live a happy life.

'My lovely Anna, God bless her, she would want them to be happy. And you mustn't worry one bit about never living up to some impossible ideal. My daughter was everything to me, but she was no angel.' Catherine laughed softly to herself. 'We paint such saints with our memories, don't we?'

Stella was lost in thinking how she'd also created saints of her parents, remembering only their lovely aspects and casting into the shadows anything less than ideal. She was spared the ordeal of feeling disloyal to them by the intercom buzzing, and she got up to press the button, only to hear heavy breathing.

'Hello, Daniel.'

'Hello, Stella,' the little boy panted. 'Guess what, guess what!'

Stella laughed. 'What, what?'

'We won! We won the cricket and I've got you a prize.'

'A prize, eh? Well you'd better come up and show it to me.'

She buzzed him in and stood waiting at the door. In a couple of minutes, Daniel raced out of the lift, waving an England cricket hat in her direction – a hat very similar to the one her father used to wear when he went fishing.

'Here's your prize, Stella,' he said. 'I've got one just the same.'

'It's a lovely prize, thank you. Let me try it on.'

'Very fetching,' whispered Bob as he passed. 'But I think he means present rather than prize.'

'No, I don't, Grandpa,' said Daniel. 'I know what a present is. This is a prize because England won.'

'Daniel, do you want some milk? Tea for everyone else?'

While Stella made tea, Daniel explored her flat. When Benedict tried to stop him, she called through and said it was fine but to keep an eye on him if he went onto the balcony.

'The balcony? Daddy, I wish we had a balcony. Can I have my milk on the balcony with you, Stella?'

'If your dad says it's all right,' she replied, carrying through a loaded tray and setting it on the table.

With permission from Benedict, she took her own mug and Daniel's milk out onto the balcony and closed the glass doors behind them. Together, they gazed up and down Abbey Road while Daniel filled her in on the cricket match, how his daddy had been good at cricket when he was a little boy, and how he was going to practise hard so he could be just as good as his father when he grew up.

'Will you come round and help me please, Stella? Sometimes on a Saturday when I'm not at school?'

'We'll have to see, Daniel. Now, do you see that white building over the road with all the people hanging around outside? It's a recording studio and lots of famous musicians record their music there.'

The door opened then and Bob came out to join them. The balcony was scarcely six feet wide, and she and Daniel were already occupying most of those six feet. Bob lifted up his grandson, took his seat and parked him on his lap. Peering over the wrought-iron railing, he pointed to the studio.

'I don't believe it,' he said. 'Daniel, look over there.'

Outside the studio, a young man in shades was walking briskly away from a sleek navy-blue car, tailed by a small crowd.

'Is that Grandma's favourite singer?' asked Daniel in an awed voice.

'I'm sure it is. That car of his costs a pretty penny and not many young men can afford a set of wheels like that.'

Daniel hopped off his grandfather's knee, rushed to the front of the balcony and yelled down to catch the man's attention. The man turned around, raised his shades and peered up at Daniel.

'Hello, it's me! My Grandma Catherine loves you. She can sing all of your songs because she knows them off by heart.'

The man cracked a wide, dazzling smile and held up one thumb. Daniel bounced up and down and Stella got up to grab him under the armpits in case he bounced himself over the edge in his excitement. The man counted the floors up and along to Stella's apartment, then he waved and was gone.

'Grandma loves him, you know,' said Daniel, 'but not more than she loves you, Grandpa.'

'Thank goodness I've still got the edge,' said Bob, 'but I have to work hard to maintain it.'

'Yes, Gramps. Grandma loves you best of all, then she loves me and then Daddy and then you, Stella, doesn't she?'

'Well, maybe.' Stella rocked her hand from side to side. 'Come on, see if you can spot anyone else.'

Bob eased his legs out in front of him and rubbed his knees. 'So, Stella, how's business?'

'Not so bad. I've just coughed up for some online advertising to bring in more custom. It's very handy being able to work remotely as the world can come to me quite easily, and it was a godsend during the pandemic.'

Daniel tapped her on the arm. 'I heard a buzz from in there.'

Puzzled, she got up and went inside, closely followed by Daniel and Bob. Catherine and Benedict were busy talking in low voices and oblivious to anything going on around them. Stella pressed the button for the intercom speaker.

'Afternoon, Stella,' said Ernie. 'A runner from the studio just dropped over with a present for the little boy on the balcony, but she said only if that was all right with his mother.'

'Hang on, Ernie.' Oh, not again. Stella wished the floor would open up and swallow her. 'Er, is that all right with you, Benedict?' she asked.

He looked slightly blank. 'Well, if you think it's all right, Stella, then that'll be fine.'

'Thanks Ernie, we're on our way down. Come on, Daniel. Let's go and see.' Together, they ran to the lift. When they reached the ground floor, the doorman was waiting with a CD.

When he saw it, Daniel's shoulders drooped.

'Oh, it's been scribbled on.'

Ernie had to put his head down to hide his laugh, but he couldn't stop his shoulders from heaving.

'We'll take it upstairs for a better look,' said Stella. 'Now say thank you to Ernie.'

'Thank you, Ernie. I've got to go now to show Grandma this scribbly CD. Bye, Ernie.'

Stella had to run to catch up with the little boy as he dashed into the lift. He ran back through her open door, red-faced with excitement, straight into Catherine's waiting arms.

'Grandma, Grandma. Look, it's that man you like. I talked to him on the balcony but it was all right because Gramps and Stella were there and I wasn't talking to strangers well not properly anyway but look he's given me this. It's a CD with a photo of him on it only it's got scribble all over it so it'll need a good scrub.'

'Daniel, sweetheart, slow down and take a breath.' Catherine accepted the gift from him. 'This isn't scribble. It's joined-up writing, and you're still learning that. It's been dedicated, you see. This writing says *To Grandma Catherine, with lots of love*. Then he's signed his name, and underneath it, there are three kisses.'

'Well, you'll definitely want the kisses, so we'd better not scrub those off.'

'We don't want to scrub any of it off. This writing makes it an extra special gift, and you must look after it carefully so you'll always remember today and you can show it to your children.'

'Don't be silly, Grandma, I'm not having any children.

I'm only seven. You have to be a grown-up to have babies. Honestly.'

'Well, you never know, Daniel. One day you might find yourself all grown up. It happens to the best of us.'

Daniel looked at his grandmother as if she'd taken leave of her senses.

'I'm never going to grow up, Grandma. I've decided.'

Catherine slipped the CD into her handbag for safe keeping. 'Anyway, Daniel, do you feel like coming home with me and Grandpa tonight?'

'What day will it be in the morning?'

'Sunday, why?'

'Are you going to make a great big Sunday dinner with Yorkshire puddings and roast beef?'

'Grandpa would be rather disappointed if I didn't.'

'I'll come then. As long as I can have three Yorkshire puddings. Daddy, you never make Sunday dinner like Grandma does.' Snuggling into Catherine's side, he looked up at her with big eyes. 'Grandma, do you still have my special pyjamas in my special bed at your house?'

'I do, darling. But now you're seven, they might be getting a bit small, so you'll need some new ones...'

She pointed to the pile of shopping bags and Daniel's brows shot up.

'For me?' He rushed over to the bags and opened them until he found a pair of summer pyjamas with cartoon aliens on the front.

'Ooh! Do these glow in the dark, Grandma?'

'You'll find out at bedtime.' She got to her feet and put on her shoes with some difficulty. 'Thank you for a delightful afternoon, Stella. We must do it again sometime soon, once my feet have returned to a more normal size.'

After kissing her on the cheek, Catherine stepped over to her son-in-law and kissed him. Bob shook hands with Benedict and Stella. Daniel kissed everyone, including his grandparents, and put his cricket hat on, ready for the journey.

They all walked down to the Telfords' car together to make sure everyone was safely packed in. Daniel had a long hug from his father and a quick kiss from Stella. Finally, with much waving and smiling, and a sweeping U-turn that made Benedict take a sharp breath, they were off. When the car had disappeared into the distance and it would have been ridiculous to wave any longer, Stella and Benedict stood quietly side by side. What had been a companionable few minutes of waving and smiling had turned into something more awkward.

Eventually, she had to speak. 'At the risk of being unoriginal, would you like to come up for some coffee?'

'Coffee, Stella?' He examined his watch. 'At this time of night?'

She laughed nervously. 'Obviously, I didn't mean *coffee* coffee.'

'Tea, then? Come on.' He put an arm around her and together they walked back towards her building. 'We need to talk.'

Ernie had made himself scarce and they waited for the lift in silence. Once inside her flat, Stella started to walk towards the kitchen but Benedict caught her shoulders and turned her around until she was facing him.

'I don't want coffee. Or tea. Look at me, Stella. I'm so sorry, but I hope you understand that I have to do this.'

He pulled her into his arms and looked into her eyes until she felt she might go cross-eyed and had to close them. Then he kissed her. And this time, there was no near-miss.

———

In the morning, Stella woke with the light streaming through her window. She felt strangely happy and it took a moment or two for her to remember the night before. It hadn't been a dream because she was nestled in a pair of bare arms and surrounded by that lovely nutmeg smell. She stirred against Benedict's chest.

'Morning, sleepyhead,' he said. 'I wondered when you'd finally wake up.'

'You mean you've been watching me?'

'Only because I left my phone in my jacket pocket. Had to alleviate the boredom somehow.'

Stella rolled her eyes, but it was wasted because she was still facing his chest.

He kissed the top of her head and murmured, 'I love you, Stella.'

At this, Stella froze against him and he held her at arm's length.

'What? What's wrong? Have I misjudged?'

'No, not at all. I love you as well, of course I do. It's just that I've spent so long wishing for this moment but also hoping it would never happen. It's all so difficult.'

'I know,' he said. 'I know what you mean, but as we've decided we love each other, and as we've er, tested the goods, we can hardly go back on it now. Look, let me give you a bit of space. I'll nip out and fetch us some croissants and organise coffee. Then we can talk about how we're going to find our way around this.'

'Thank you. My brain works better after caffeine. I might grab a quick shower while you're out. Try the high street, near the brasserie. Can you find your way back there?'

'Not without my map app, I can't. Won't be long.'

―――――

When Stella emerged from the shower, wrapped in her bathrobe, Benedict had set out a pot of coffee and a plateful of freshly made croissants on the balcony. She joined him at the little table and sipped her coffee while he wolfed down a piece of pain au chocolat.

'Sorry, do you want some?'

'You can have it all,' she said. 'I've no appetite.'

Leaning over, he kissed her and went back to wolfing down pastries.

'That's no good, you'll need to keep your strength up. As soon as you've replenished your energy, I'm carrying you back to bed because we need to have an in-depth discussion about the effects of the Saturn return. You must be about due your first one. I went through mine years ago, so if you need any tips, I'm your man.'

'Where did you learn about the Saturn return?' Stella laughed, delighted at the prospect of spending a long Sunday morning in bed discussing astrology with Benedict.

'Oh, research,' he said. 'I'm not just a pretty face, you know.'

'So, with your new-found interest in astrology, don't you think it's time you told me your date, time and place of birth and let me analyse you properly?'

'Sorry, Ms McElhone, but that information is restricted and can only be divulged to family members, so I'm afraid there's another conversation that we need to have first.'

Epilogue

Stella McElhone stepped off the river bus at Greenwich Pier and walked towards the park, her dark hair swinging behind her. Her destination was only about half a mile away, but if she didn't get a move on, she'd be late and make a bad entrance.

Of course, Ernie was not exactly the fastest of walkers at the best of times, but the others could hardly start without them. Even though it was only November, it was chilly, so she was glad to have her mother's cream wrap for warmth, and she pulled it more tightly around her shoulders.

As Stella and Ernie made their way up the hill to the Royal Observatory, Catherine and Bob Telford walked towards them. Catherine was dressed in a slub silk lemon suit, complete with matching shoes, handbag and hat. The mischievous Mrs Telford had known exactly whose wedding she was buying that outfit for. Her eyes sparkled and Bob seemed to be having trouble with a lump in his throat. Behind them was Daniel, jumping up and down with excitement.

Catherine took Stella's hands between her own. 'My dear Stella, you look so beautiful.'

Bob bent and kissed her on the cheek.

'I wish you'd have let me pick the pair of you up in the car instead of doing battle with public transport.'

Stella shook her head. 'Thank you, Bob, but I wanted the journey to be the same as the first time I came here and met Benedict – Tube delays, river bus and all.' She turned to the porter from her apartment block. 'But I'm sorry for making you endure it, Ernie.'

'Wouldn't have had it any other way, mate. It's a great honour being asked to stand for you, especially seeing as I've none of my own.'

Catherine gave her a quick wink before Bob escorted his wife indoors and Stella blew Daniel a kiss. Ernie held out his arm and Stella hooked her own into it. As they walked into the planetarium, her eyes met Benedict's. He was standing at the front in a grey morning suit and although his eyes were usually a pale-blue, they were dark as he watched her walk towards him.

The bride wore a long sheath of cream silk and carried a small spray of red roses and honeysuckle, with matching buds sewn into her hair. She smiled at her husband-to-be, glad to have Ernie at her side for support. The registrar looked up and beckoned the trio to the front as otherworldly music started to play. Stella recognised 'Neptune, the Mystic' from *The Planets*. She smiled, amazed that Benedict knew about Neptune ruling Pisces. Gustav Holst was rumoured to have been a keen astrologer, and Benedict's thoughtfulness was deeply touching.

Walking slowly, Stella and Ernie arrived in front of the registrar. When she asked who was giving Stella away, Ernie proudly took Stella's hand and passed it to Benedict before stepping back to take a seat. Catherine held Bob's hand as she dabbed at her eyes.

Daniel, as best man, was dressed in a replica of his father's morning suit, complete with tails and tie. He passed the ring to the minister at the appropriate time, accompanied by oohs and aahs from the small congregation. Then he stepped back to stand with his Aunt Miranda, who put an arm around him and smiled happily at her brother and sister-in-law-to-be.

As Stella swore her vows, she gazed up at Professor Redman, the man she was pledging the rest of her life to, and noticed that the overhead lights had been dimmed at some point so they were now surrounded by the night sky, lit with hundreds of constellations. She kissed her husband under a starry sky, to the sound of loud cheers and clapping.

Daniel groaned in disgust. 'I hate kissing. I'm never going to kiss girls when I grow up.'

Catherine hugged him. 'You might change your mind one day, Daniel. Oh, weddings always make me so happy.'

She sniffled into a lace handkerchief while Daniel looked at her, quite perplexed.

'But you're not happy at all, Grandma. You've cried the whole time.'

Catherine, unable to speak, squeezed her grandson until he protested and she reluctantly let him go. Bob explained to Daniel that Grandma was perfectly happy, and that sometimes when people were very happy, it could make them cry. The best man's expression suggested that he remained to be convinced.

After a small reception held at the brasserie in St John's Wood, Stella, Benedict and Daniel drove off in the mustard sports car, which was draped with cream satin ribbons. After a couple of hours, they pulled into the churchyard where Anna was buried. The little family walked to her grave, and Daniel tucked his buttonhole rose into the vase at the foot of her headstone.

'Hello, Mummy. Here's my flower from the wedding. Daddy and Stella got married today. I wish you were here to see me in my smart suit. Grandma says I look even more handsome than Daddy and Grandpa put together.'

He hopped from one foot to another then ran to his father's side.

'Hello, Anna,' Benedict began, holding his son and his new wife close. 'This is Stella. You'd have both got on like a house on fire. I'm never going to forget you, but I know you'd want me to be happy.'

Stella crouched down to lay her wedding bouquet at Anna's gravestone before standing up again.

'Hello, Anna. I've heard so much about you from your loved ones and want you to know that I'll do everything in my power to make Benedict and Daniel happy.'

She looked down at the epitaph, saddened at the short interval between the date of Anna's birth and the date of her death. Her hand instinctively went to her womb. Seeing the movement, Benedict stepped forwards and turned her slowly to face him, a question written in his eyes. Unable to find any words, she nodded, and he drew his wife and son close.

Darkness had fallen and all the stars had started to pop out across the miles of velvet sky. Stella looked up at her old friends. The stars had always been there throughout her life, and in one way or another, they'd brought her and Benedict together. She looked to the sky to find her mother and father. Silently, she told them her news.

I'm part of a family again.

Also by Hannah Keens

Laying Down the Law (Book 2)

Can an environmental lawyer and an aristocratic landowner end their legal battle and find love? Or are they just courting disaster?

After Miranda Redman's marriage breaks down, she throws herself into her work. Saving the planet and social justice are her twin passions. So she is only too pleased to take on a case fighting a tyrannical toff who wants to build on common land.

Hayden Carrington may be a peer of the realm, but his estate is crumbling, and he needs to develop some land to save his family and the people who work for them. It's all going swimmingly until the villagers get lawyered up and he finds himself toe to toe with Miranda in court.

In the sequel to *Meantime in Greenwich*, discover how Miranda got to be so frosty, and whether the eleventh earl of Ridler Norgard is the man to melt her heart.

(Watch out for Stella, Benedict and Daniel, who are only lending a helping hand and not interfering at all.)

Can't Marry, Won't Marry (Book 3)

An ancient legacy means Lady Eve Carrington can't marry. Damian Webster won't marry after a jilting.

Can a quirky aristocrat and the heir to a family fortune outrun love, or will they trip and fall heart-first? Find out in this heartwarming romantic comedy.

(Hayden Carrington will be on hand to look out for his little sister, Eve, ably assisted by the entire Redman family.)

Author note

Author website and newsletter

For more information about my writing or to subscribe to my newsletter, please visit hannahkeens.com.

Stella's day out in Covent Garden

When Stella has her day out in Covent Garden, she visits 'a quaint emporium selling mystical paraphernalia'. While Meredith and the shopkeeper are my own inventions, the emporium was inspired by the shop, Mysteries, which is sadly no longer there.

I first visited this shop in 1989, when it was sited on Monmouth Street by Shaftesbury Avenue. I used to go there often as a treat and picked up some excellent books over the years. Mysteries later moved to nearby Short's Gardens and more recently shifted to being an online presence only. If you'd like to look around the old shop, you'll find a link on my blog where you can step inside and browse.

Useful astrology courses and resources

Stella learned astrology from her late mother, but I learned it by reading a wide range of books in my youth and by later attending classes at the Faculty of Astrological Studies in London. In those days, getting to class meant an atmospheric evening walk past the high prison wall of HMP Pentonville, but nowadays classes are held in Bloomsbury as well as online.

Stella goes to Chelsea to meet the Constellations (a rather mean-spirited group made up by me), but you'll find lists of more welcoming local groups on the Astrological Association website.

Of course, neither of these august organisations are responsible for any astrology-related errors in this book. I claim sole responsibility for those.

Stella's flat

For a few months in the late eighties, I was fortunate enough to live on Abbey Road in St John's Wood, in a pleasant flat overlooking the recording studio. Despite frequently lurking on the balcony, unlike Stella, I never once spotted anyone famous coming or going.

The Astronomers

The astronomers are all fictional, as is the skinflint Saturn Committee, who insisted on taking their own wine/paint-stripper to the lecture at the planetarium. Of course, the real-life Peter Harrison Planetarium serves only the highest quality wines at its events. Information about Saturn's vanishing rings came from NASA's website. Once again, any errors are all my own work.

BV - #0185 - 281024 - C0 - 198/129/11 - PB - 9781915421173 - Matt Lamination